Don't Kill the Messenger

a novel

by Joel Pierson

iUniverse, Inc.
New York   Bloomington

DON'T KILL THE MESSENGER
A Novel

iUniverse books may be ordered through booksellers or by contacting:

iUniverse
1663 Liberty Drive
Bloomington, IN 47403
www.iuniverse.com
1-800-Authors (1-800-288-4677)

ISBN: 978-1-4401-3976-5 (sc)
ISBN: 978-1-4401-3975-8 (hc)

Printed in the United States of America

iUniverse rev. date: 5/8/2009

Acknowledgments

Profuse thanks to my writing group, Jamie, Melissa, Holly, and Christy, for taking the journey with me, chapter by chapter. Your eagerness to see more and your willingness to rein me in when things went astray made a huge difference.

And thanks, of course, to Dana, who encouraged me to take this one all the way. If it weren't for her, I wouldn't even know what a key deer is.

About the Author

Joel Pierson is the author of numerous award-winning plays for audio and stage, including *French Quarter, The Children's Zoo, The Vigil, Cow Tipping,* and *Mourning Lori.* He also co-authored the novelization of *French Quarter.* How he has time to write is anyone's guess, as he spends his days as editorial manager at the world's largest print-on-demand publishing company. Additionally, he is artistic director of Mind's Ear Audio Productions, the producers of several popular audio theatre titles and the official audio guided tour of Arlington National Cemetery. If that weren't enough, he also writes for the newspaper and a local lifestyles magazine in his hometown of Bloomington, Indiana. He stays grounded and relatively sane with the help of his wife (and frequent co-author) Dana, and his three ridiculously loving dogs.

Chapter 1

It began, as it always begins, with pain. Two days ago, in the privacy and comfort of my home, I suffered a searing firestorm of pain that started in my right leg and worked its way up through my abdomen and into my chest, radiating out through both arms. When it struck, I dropped to my hands and knees and struggled to stay focused. Because I knew that with the agony came vital information. It was how I learned about Rebecca.

My life has not been my own for almost two years; I go where I am sent. I don't know who is sending me or even why I've been chosen. All I have are the circumstances of the moment as each new day begins. This day's circumstances find me in a car, a gold-colored Chrysler Sebring convertible. It's not mine, but it's not stolen—a rental car I picked up in Maryland. I'm the good guy, if there is such a thing; I know they're a little hard to find these days. But I like to think that my intentions are good, even if plenty of people think I'm crazy or I'm scamming them. In America circa the new millennium, cynicism has become a cash crop.

I'm driving south on a little strip of road called U.S. 1, down to Key West, Florida. I've never been, but courtesy of the information I received, I know the way, turn by turn. It's a piece of knowledge that saves some money and some hassle. The rental companies want twelve bucks a day to rent a GPS for the car. I remember when they used to give you a free map to where you were going.

Most of the time, no matter how far I have to go, I drive. I make a conscious decision not to fly. It's not because of fear, but rather a question of control. Flights can be delayed or canceled, airplanes can be re-routed to unexpected airports, but the road is always open. And if I'm late for an appointment, somebody could die.

It's early September and it's dark out; just past 9:00 at night, I am still about thirty miles from Key West. U.S. 1 is a straight shot, an asphalt line, snaking its way to the southernmost point in the continental United States. Side streets jut out to the left and right, taking travelers to the Atlantic Ocean or the Gulf of Mexico, depending on which way they turn.

There's a decent amount of humidity in the air tonight; an indecent amount might be a better description of it. Even without the heat of the sun, the moisture makes the air feel very close, even with the top down on the Chrysler and the wind moving through my hair. I'm outdoors and I still feel like I want to open a window. But I paid an extra $30 a day for the convertible, and unless it's raining or the damn thing is parked, that top is staying down.

Then there's the crackling. When I first heard it, about ten miles back, I didn't know what it was or where it was coming from. At first, I thought something was short circuiting on the car. Then I slowed down and looked up at the high-tension wires paralleling the road, and there it was—the crackling. Like something out of an old science fiction movie, where the killer robot is staggering toward its defeat. The dampness is reacting with the power lines, resulting in a disturbing constant buzz, and that buzz is traveling across those wires, making it sound like they are leaking electricity, which might drop on my head at any second. It almost makes me want to put the top up.

Almost.

Instead I make an effort to ignore the crackling.

A mile or two down the road, the speed limit drops to thirty-five. Apparently the road crosses through a wildlife refuge for something called key deer, an endangered species of animal little and cute enough to warrant not just protecting it but showing it off to the public. I drive through at the reduced speed, irritating drivers behind me who clearly could give two craps for any species—endangered or not—and impatiently ride my ass until such time as they can pass me at about fifty. Halfway through the sanctuary, I'm free of ass-riders and alone with the night air. I see the deer ahead at the side of the road, about fifty yards, maybe a hundred yards up—hell, I don't know. Spatial relations were never my thing. But there he is, as little and cute as I expected, and wandering squarely into the middle of my lane.

Fortunately, this isn't the story of a car crash. I'm going slowly enough that I can bring the Chrysler to a full stop a good five feet from the deer, who—in a moment too cliché to appreciate—stands staring into my headlights. Since he doesn't seem too intent on moving, I turn on my hazard lights and sit looking at him. I honk the horn; he's unimpressed.

After a full minute of this standoff—and for reasons I don't really even understand—I say, "Hi there."

The furry little beast looks at me for a moment, then opens his mouth a bit, and I hear the word "Hey."

Less jarred by this than I should be, I continue the conversation. "You hungry or something? I have Funyuns."

"Didn't you read the sign?" the deer asks. "You're not supposed to feed us. It's the number-one cause of road kills among my species—drivers hit us when we stand by the road, getting fed."

"Not to be pedantic," I chime in, "but I suspect the number-two cause of road kills among your species would be standing in the middle of the street."

"Touché," he says calmly. "Don't worry. I'll move in a minute."

I ask the next obvious question, only dreading the answer a little. "Is there a particular reason you're talking to me?"

"I'm not, really," he answers in that same calm tone. "You're projecting. You're tired, a little lonely, and thinking about what you have to do tonight. You needed someone to give you a message, and I was the only one around."

What's most notable to me is how reasonable it all sounds. "So what's the message?" I ask. If my diminutive conversation partner is right and I'm really just projecting, then I already know the answer. This will be the acid test.

"Don't fall in love," the little fuzzball retorts.

Bingo, we have a winner. Still, I can't help baiting him. "Ever, or just tonight?"

"Tonight," he answers. "With her."

"Wasn't planning on it," I say, trying to sound nonchalant, but feeling overwhelmingly chalant.

"That's good," he says, trotting to the side of the road. "Drive carefully."

I turn off the hazards and resume my previous pace southward. *Don't fall in love.* Didn't the Tubes tell me the same thing back in 1983? Yeah, she's a beauty, all right. Or so I imagine, since I haven't even met her yet.

Forty-five minutes later, I pull into the city limits of Key West, Florida. I've long since missed the sunset, the nightly excuse for festivity and debauchery that brings the locals and the tourists together at Mallory Square in the middle of town. Not that the debauchery ends at dark; it goes well into the night most nights. And I'm headed for one of its favorite haunts.

The place is called Gulf Breezes, and it has an unassuming storefront on Caroline Street, tucked away with the restaurants, bars, and shops. Out front, two girls in exotic costumes are handing out cards to passersby. "All Nude Dancers," the cards say. "First Mixed Drink $1.00 Off With This Card."

One of the pair smiles at me as she hands me a card. "Come on in, hon?" she offers. "See the nicest girls in the Florida Keys?"

"Why not," I reply, letting her think she's talked me into it. Who knows, maybe they work on commission.

Inside, the place is loud. Music pours from speakers that seem to be on every wall. Black lights cast an unnatural glow on every surface, turning everything that's white a shade of green—even people's teeth. I've never been in a strip club before. Honest. "Titty bars," my friend John calls them, but from the looks of the dancer on stage, the show doesn't stop at the waistline. The stage is in the middle of the room, raised about three feet off the ground, and sporting two metal poles, one at each end. On it, a single girl, maybe twenty-one years old, moves in time to the music. I must have walked in toward the end of her routine, because she is stark naked save for a lace garter, displaying what God gave her, for the crowd to see.

The place isn't seedy, as far as I can tell, though I have no basis of comparison. It doesn't reek of alcohol, or anything else for that matter. The clientele seem well-behaved, and the floor isn't dirty or sticky. It's a good start.

There are tables set up away from the stage, and most of these are occupied, primarily by men, though a few have female companionship. It takes a special woman to say, "Sure, hon, let's go knock back a few at the strip club tonight." The bar is also well-populated, though the crowd there seems much more interested in booze than boobs. Then there's the front-row seating, a row of chairs surrounding the stage itself. Only a few men are seated around it, all of them staring up at the dancer as she swings herself around the pole in a move that should be considered an Olympic sport. The ratings would certainly go up in a big damn hurry, I'll tell you that much.

I make my way to one of the front-row seats. The "tip rail" I soon learn it's called. All the men there have stacks of one-dollar bills in front of them. Periodically, one of them tents a dollar—its white areas greener than its green areas, courtesy of the black light—and puts it on the edge of the stage. I watch in fascination as the dancer responds. She slinks her way over to the patron on her hands and knees, then runs her fingers through his hair. I can't get a bead on what he's thinking. Outside, he's completely calm, but inside … Is he on fire or just too numb to feel it?

My amazement continues as she contorts her body, placing her lower extremities on either side of the man's head and displaying herself in a manner that would allow the customer to perform a Pap smear, if he were so inclined. Apparently disinclined, he simply stares at her as if he's seeing a woman for the first time. His hands, curiously enough, stay almost glued to the edge of the stage. *House rules,* I think to myself, *looky but no touchy. Makes sense.*

She then gets back on her knees and eases right up to him. In a moment that ranks up there with college in terms of completing my education, I watch as she presses the stranger's face between her breasts, going so far as to brush his lips with each nipple. She then stands before him and holds her garter away from her thigh. I see that it is stuffed with money, and she invites him to add to the pile. He takes a single dollar, folds it in half, and tucks it in with the others. She smiles and says, "Thanks, hon," competing with the music.

A dollar. Even with the economy in chaos, this man got … Holy shit, no wonder the terrorists want us all dead.

My thoughts are interrupted by a touch on my shoulder. Surprised, I turn around to see a waitress dressed in lingerie, seeking my attention. "What can I get ya?" she asks pleasantly.

"Oh, I'm fine, thanks," I tell her.

"One-drink minimum," she says with a gently apologetic look.

"Can I just get a Sprite?"

"Sure, that's fine. I'll be right back."

She retreats to the bar and the current song ends. The dancer on stage gathers her costume, as an unseen DJ camps it up. "Give it up for Chantelle!" From the looks on some of the faces in the room, I suspect that a few men have done precisely that. Given the pervasiveness of the black light, I only hope they did so discreetly.

The DJ continues, "Isn't she great, guys? Don't forget, our girls work for your tips, so those of you at the tip rail, give generously and you shall receive. The bar is open and serving up all your favorites. Don't forget to tip your waitress. Comin' to the stage next, let's make some noise for Fantasia."

A few of the more intoxicated patrons do in fact make some noise … some *sort* of noise for Fantasia. Onto the stage sashays a young black woman in a bright red latex outfit. I had silently hoped she would come out in a sorcerer's cap and robe, in homage to her namesake film, but alas. I watch as she begins her dance, and I smile noncommittally in her direction. At that moment, my waitress returns, carrying a plastic sixteen-ounce cup filled with Sprite-flavored ice and a little bubbly clear liquid. "Four dollars, hon," she says.

I hand her a twenty. "Can I have the change in singles?"

"Of course," she says pleasantly. She gives me sixteen one-dollar bills, and I give her back two of them.

"Thanks," she says, genuinely grateful. "I'll be back around if you need anything." *Nicest girls in the Florida Keys.* Everyone's polite, I'll have to give them that.

Up on stage, Fantasia is making the rounds. Slowly, very deliberately, she finds the precise right moment to ease out of each article of clothing. Gradually she reveals her body for the crowd—an arm, a leg (well, two of each, actually, lest it sound like she is an amputee). When the moment is right, she pours herself out of the top of her costume, and her breasts emerge; small, dark, with the firmness of youth. She has a dancer's body.

At this point, the dollar bills start to come out. Fantasia visits those who offer, teasing a bit, touching a bit. A minute more, and she sheds the last garment: a bright red latex thong. I do a double take worthy of 1930s slapstick comedy when I see that she is sporting jewelry in her genital region. A silver chain six inches in length dangles from a piercing that—despite my lack of that equipment—looks like it's gotta hurt.

It's time. I place a dollar bill conspicuously on the stage, and Fantasia pays me a visit. Despite years of being told that it's rude to stare, I'm mesmerized by the chain. It looks like something that the family butler would pull to bring coal down the chute. She sees me staring, inasmuch as she isn't legally blind.

"You like my voodoo kitty?" she purrs.

Desperately as the moment calls for a witty retort—something about voodoo or chains or butlers—all I can manage is, "It's nice."

She slinks over to me, squats down, and actually picks up the dollar bill with a body part I would never have considered capable until this moment. I resist the urge to applaud. Fantasia then spirits the dollar away and gets down on all fours before me, looking me right in the face. "So what's your name?"

"Bill," I say. It isn't. I smile to myself. "Not much of a Tina Turner fan, are you?"

She is genuinely puzzled, the musical reference probably predating her birth. "Huh?"

"You know ... 'Private ...' Inside joke. My fault."

She dismisses it quickly and proceeds to dispense the amount of performance that she will offer for a dollar. A few twists and turns, and the prehensile voodoo genitalia make another appearance in all their chained glory. I'm intrigued; I know my friend John would be in the throes of a mild seizure at the sight of this. He leans toward the exotic.

Contorting again, Fantasia brings her breasts forward toward my face. Rather than gently rubbing them on me, she thrusts them forward until my nose and mouth are wedged between them. I taste baby powder; it tastes like it smells. "Choke on them!" she says playfully, although I detect something in her tone that suggests that if I were to actually asphyxiate, she wouldn't weep long. Curious customer service attitude. I'm glad the waitresses at Denny's don't adopt a similar one. Though it makes for an amusing mental image as I'm waiting for the oxygen supply to return.

She pulls away, offers a cryptic smile, and says, "See ya around … *Bill*." I think she knows it's not my name.

Before she can approach the next patron, I offer the question I came here to ask, the reason I placed the dollar bill on stage in the first place: "Is Rebecca dancing tonight?"

She looks surprised to hear it. We've clearly never met before, and she doesn't recognize me as a regular, and here I am asking a question she would expect from a frequent patron. Deciding that I'm not visibly dangerous, she says, "She's up next."

"Thank you."

I pause for a healthy swig of my Sprite-and-water cocktail, with its baby-powder chaser, and I watch Fantasia perform a nearly identical ritual on a Hispanic man in his fifties, right down to the choking comment. *At least it wasn't personal,* I think.

Three or four more minutes pass; Fantasia's *symphonie vaginique* ends, and she makes her way off the stage. "Isn't she amazing?" the DJ asks rhetorically. A few audience members offer sounds to the affirmative. "Gulf Breezes is glad you're here, and don't forget, we're having a special on private dances tonight. Normally forty dollars, for the next hour, you can get a dance all to yourself with the girl of your choice for just *twwwwwwenty dollars*. Don't be shy, guys. These girls want to perform for you. And comin' to the stage right now—she's too sexy for her shirt, so it won't be on her for long. Please welcome Rebecca!"

Unsurprisingly, the tedium of "I'm Too Sexy" pours forth from the speakers, but before I can even roll my eyes, I see her. Rebecca. The reason I'm here. The reason I rented a car and drove 1,200 miles. And wouldn't you know it, she's a beauty.

But don't fall in love …

"Like I have time for that anyway," I say quietly to the warning lyric before it can become a full-fledged earworm.

Rebecca Traeger, all of twenty-one years old. She has light brown hair. I have no idea what color her eyes are. I would guess green, but thanks to the lighting, the same can be said of her teeth. She looks through me; we've never met, so there's no reason for her to do anything else.

Part of me wants to look away as she begins to undress, feeling like I owe her the courtesy of averting my gaze. But I realize that I would draw too much attention to myself by doing that. And besides, I'd really like to see this girl naked.

The music doesn't lie; she *is* too sexy for the oversized white shirt she discards on a corner of the stage. As time goes on, I realize that she is similarly too sexy for her shoes, stockings, and G-string. A few intricate dance moves later, I've seen about every side of her there is to see, short of having an MRI. I place a dollar bill on the stage. It's time.

Seeing the dollar, she dances over to my direction. I briefly contemplate the potential intimacy that dollar could buy me, but before she can put anything of hers near anything of mine, I ask, "Can I have a private dance?"

She smiles, likely more at the revenue than the rendezvous. "Sure. I'll come see you after my set is over."

Before I can thank her, she is running her fingers through my hair and brushing my cheek with one breast. At the moment, I am grateful for the darkness that hits me at waist level.

Somewhere, thirty miles to the north, I sense that a deer is shaking its head in disappointment.

Chapter 2

Rebecca finishes her set and secures the dollar bills she has collected. It's an impressive stack; she's good and it pays. It pays very well, which means that she won't like what I'm going to tell her; but I have to tell her if I hope to get any sleep. She approaches me. "Fantasia told me someone at the rail was asking for me. Was that you?"

"Yes."

"Have I seen you before?"

"No," I answer, "you haven't."

"Then how did you—"

I interrupt. "Can we talk where it's quieter?"

She acknowledges the intrusiveness of the music and the bar ambiance, and motions for me to follow her to a back room. The sign over the door says "Enchantment," but the décor inside fails to enchant on many levels. The dark gray carpeting looks like it hasn't been changed since the Carter administration. The plush chairs are newer, obviously necessitated by frequent use. I am relieved not to see a bed in the room, nor anything else that might lead to an awkward discussion of what twenty dollars could buy. Though I suspect I would be very sad if that little money could secure anything of that nature.

I hold out twenty dollars, but she hesitates before accepting it. "How did you know to ask for me?" she says.

"I'm here because I have to talk to you," I answer.

For a moment, she bristles. "If you're a cop, you can leave now, because there's nothing illegal going on."

I offer a half-smile. It's a reasonable assumption. "I'm not a cop, and I'm not here to ask you for anything illegal, immoral, or anything like that. I'm here because I have a message to give you."

"In that case …" She takes the twenty from my hand, then pauses to ask, "Who's the message from?"

"I don't know," I tell her honestly.

"Well, who sent you here? How did they know where I'd be?"

"Nobody actually sent me." By now, I should have this part of the explanation down cold, but every time I say it, it sounds as impossible to me as it does to the person hearing it. "Can we sit? This is easier if we sit."

She sits in one of the plush chairs and I sit opposite her. "What I'm going to tell you will sound impossible but it's true, and it's important that you believe me when I tell you that I don't want or need anything from you. I just have to give you this message, then I'll leave and you never have to hear from me again."

"Okay …" she says, looking unsure if she should be creeped out by this prologue.

"Rebecca, you need to leave here. You need to leave this job and go back to college the first chance you get. It's not safe for you in Key West anymore."

There is silence as she looks intently at me. Any woman in her right mind would be extremely wary of a strange man who walked into her place of business, called her aside, and made such a statement about her life. And Rebecca Traeger is most definitely in her right mind. She starts with the logical assumption.

"My father sent you here."

"No. As far as I know, your father doesn't even know where you are."

"My mother, then."

"No, not her either."

She is getting agitated at my lack of answers. "Well, *who* then?"

"I don't know," I say sharply. "God, Fate, the universe. Call it what you want. All I know is that two days ago, I got information about you in my mind. In my memory, I guess you could call it. It's like I remembered things about you, when I'd never met you, never heard of you, never even known your name. And I got that message, and the overpowering need to give it to you. If I didn't give it to you, I would suffer from blinding headaches and insomnia and nausea so bad, I couldn't keep food down. So I drove here, Rebecca. Twelve hundred miles, right to the place where you work, to tell you not to work here anymore. And because I did, I'll be able to eat and sleep and live, until the next time I get a message about someone else I've never met. And then I'll have to go and find them, and tell them something unbelievable about themselves, and get the same expression on their face that I see on yours. One I've seen about ninety-five times in the last two years since this all started."

Many seconds pass and she just stares at me, trying to find the scheme in it, the scam in it. Trying to find a way this could hurt her. Her eyes say that she can't find it, and she wants to believe what I'm saying, but there's no earthly way. In the quiet of the room, she utters a single word: "How?"

"I don't know," I tell her honestly. "There's no science fiction explanation, no near-death experience or fire or car crash or anything to explain it. I just woke up one day and knew I had to warn a friend about something that was going to happen to him, so I did. And he did what I told him to do, and that thing didn't happen."

"Are you always right?"

"I don't know that either. Most of the time, I deliver the message and don't stick around to see what happens. But I think I'm right. Otherwise, what would be the point of doing all this?"

"So ..." she says, still trying to make sense of it, "this is ... your job?"

"No. Jobs pay. I don't get any money for this. It's just what I do."

"If it doesn't pay, how do you make a living?"

"I have money," I explain. "A lot of money that I didn't earn and probably don't deserve. Do you know what LEDs are?"

"LEDs?"

"It stands for light-emitting diode. It's the little red or blue or green light on your phone, your DVD player, your coffeemaker. Well, my father helped invent the LED, and every time one was put into anything, anywhere in the world, he got a fraction of a penny for it.

When he died, I continued to get that royalty, and I will for the rest of my life."

She thinks about it for a moment. "There must be billions of them in the world."

"Yeah."

"So you're rich?"

"I have more money than I need. It's what I live on. I have a house, but I'm almost never there. I don't have a fancy car; I prefer rental cars so I don't have to keep them up. I move around. I do this, I go home, I get the next message, and I move around again."

I see belief starting to linger in her expression, and I am relieved. Too often, I'm chased off or worse by people who think I'm trying to scam them or threaten them or extort money. Rebecca believes what I still have trouble believing myself.

"You help people just to help them," she says in quiet wonder. "I didn't think that existed."

"I didn't either," I admit.

All of a sudden, realization hits her, and her expression of wonder turns instantly to fear. "Wait a minute," she says. "You said I have to leave here. Is something bad going to happen to me if I don't?"

"Yes."

"What? What's going to happen? What?"

"I don't have the details."

"What do you mean you don't have the details? You can't just tell me I have to uproot my life and leave and not tell me why."

"Rebecca, if I knew, I would tell you. The message wasn't specific. It just said you have to leave here and go back to college."

"That's in Ohio," she says. "I haven't been back there in two years …"

I stand. The message is delivered, and her fear is making me uncomfortable. Best if I leave now.

"You're going?" she asks, the fear evident in her voice.

"I should."

"How long do … When do I have to leave here?"

"The sooner the better. That's all I know."

She looks like she is about to cry, and I don't think I have the emotional strength to see her do that. "I don't even know your name," she says, sounding very vulnerable.

I defy tradition, disregard my better judgment, and tell her the truth. "I'm Tristan," I say.

"Tristan." She repeats it for no reason I can discern.

"Good luck, Rebecca. I hope everything will be all right."

Without another word, I make my way out of Enchantment, and back to the main room of Gulf Breezes. Rebecca follows me out of the room. Someone new is dancing on the stage; I pay no attention. The job is done, and it's time for me to leave. I'm hungry, I'm anxious, and even though I swear to myself every single time that this time is going to be different—something in Rebecca's face or voice has gotten to me and allowed me to care about whether or not she follows my instructions. I need to get out of here before I let that care get to me.

All I can see is the exit back onto Caroline Street, a portal to my freedom from loud music, black light, physical and emotional nudity, and the burden of knowing I've just turned a young woman's life upside down. Thirty feet, twenty, fifteen, twelve, six, three, then out.

Someone says to me, "Thanks for ..." but I don't stick around long enough to hear the end of the sentence. Outside, it's still close to eighty degrees, and the humidity is equally high, but to me, the relief feels like I've stepped into an early spring breeze. I bring my hands to my temples and run my fingers through my hair, closing my eyes as I work to get enough air in my lungs.

It is only after thirty seconds of this that I turn around and realize that Rebecca has followed me out of the club and is standing behind me on the sidewalk. She looks at me, probably confused by the severity of my reaction.

I'm surprised to see her standing there, staring at me. "Hi," I say. *Not brilliant, but a start.*

"So where are we going?" she asks.

"We ... who, we?" *Even less brilliant.* "We, us, we?" *Toastmasters, here I come.*

"You can't just come into my life, tell me I have to quit my job and move five states away ..."

"Four," I correct.

"Whatever! You can't just do that and walk away."

15

"I do it all the time," I admit sheepishly.

"Well, you shouldn't, Tristan! I'm scared here, and I don't know what to do or how I'm going to get there, or anything. I don't need you to take care of me or protect me. I just need a ride."

This has never happened to me before. In the past, I've always made such a hasty retreat, I've never stuck around for the aftermath of what can be devastating news. There have been times when the recipient disregarded what I said, and I read the news story later about the consequences. But this is the first time I've stood and faced the part I've tried so hard not to face. Now I'm the one who's naked, stripped bare by my lack of a good answer to her request.

"If I said 'I work alone,' what would that make me?" I ask.

"The biggest douchebag in Florida," she replies.

"There's some pretty tough competition for that title, too, isn't there?"

"Yeah."

I can't believe I'm doing this. "One ride," I say. "Right to Ohio. We're not partners or anything."

"I don't want to be your partner," she says. "I just need the fastest way away from here, away from whatever it is that whoever it is says I need to get away from, and the fastest way is you."

"Okay."

"Okay? I can come with you?"

"Yeah, I guess you can. Do you need to go in there, talk to the manager, give your notice?"

"Yeah," she says, "just a sec."

She walks back to the front door of Gulf Breezes and holds it open. "Morty!" she calls out.

"Yeah, what?" a man's voice replies from behind the bar.

"I quit!" she announces amiably.

"Okay," Morty calls out. "See ya!"

She closes the door and looks at me. "Lead the way," she says.

Chapter 3

I had parked in the closest available parking spot to the club, so we walk the four blocks back to the car at a good pace. The lack of details in my message to Rebecca leaves us both uncertain whether the danger is ten days away or ten minutes away. Whichever it is, I've seen enough of Key West in any case. I didn't bank on leaving town accompanied, but now that I am, I have to make the best of it on the long drive to Ohio. I'll have to call the rental car company now, extend the agreement, and change the drop-off location.

Ohio. Been a while.

"Could you slow down a little?" She interrupts my thoughts. "It's hard to follow you in these shoes."

"Take 'em off, then," I say. "Should be a procedure you're familiar with." I regret it immediately. She didn't deserve that. As she stops to remove the shoes, I apologize. "I'm not what you'd call a people person," I explain.

"Yeah, I've noticed," she says. As we start walking again, she asks, "Do you ever give people *good* news?"

"It's not why I'm sent. I figure the good news is when they listen to my instructions and get to see another day."

We make it back to the Chrysler, and I open it up and put the top down. She gets in quickly, looking around. "Do you think they saw us?"

"I don't know. I don't even know if there is a 'they.' The message didn't say. All I know is you're supposed to leave Key West and go back to college."

"God, I still can't believe this. I just met you twenty minutes ago, and now I'm supposed to drive across the country with you. How do I know you're not a pervert who's going to drive me into a cornfield and rape me to death?"

"Okay," I reply, starting the car, "first off, the driving you across the country part was *your* idea. As you recall, I was prepared to leave here without you, which is probably what made you believe that I'm not a rapist pervert—which, by the way, I'm not. And secondly, there are no cornfields in southern Florida. So, apart from that little agricultural detail, you have two choices: You can trust me and we can drive to Ohio or you can get out here and do whatever you would have done if I hadn't walked into your life."

She thinks about it for several seconds as the car idles. She searches my eyes for truth, for honesty. "You're not here to hurt me?"

I shake my head.

"And you don't want anything from me?"

"No. Not even gas money." I realize, "That's unusual in your life, isn't it?"

She nods.

"I'm sorry to hear that." And I genuinely am.

After a moment, she asks, "Can we stop at my place for a few minutes?"

Without any good reason, my response is suspicious: "Why? What's at your place?"

She gestures to her outfit. "Umm, clothes? Some stuff to take along. I can't drive to Ohio looking like an extra from *Showgirls*."

"Okay. Tell me where to go."

"You mean you don't know where I live, the way you know where I work?"

It is bordering on interrogation, and I am in no mood. "No, because going to your home wasn't in the plans or the assignment. So if you want to get there, some directions might be more helpful than you're being right now."

My tone is scolding, and it silences her. Though an apology isn't formally offered, it resides in her next statement. "Take a right at the corner."

She lives alone in a small apartment. It isn't fancy, but it's far from run-down. She clearly makes enough money to afford comfortable living conditions. No car, though. No high-end electronics either. It makes me wonder if she's deep in debt or saving up for something. Maybe both. There's a time and a place to ask her about it, but this is neither. Since I delivered the message, she's been edgy; understandably so. Now, as I stand in her living room, she flits about the place, grabbing two soft-sided bags and filling them with essentials. She then grabs a more practical outfit: a pair of shorts, a comfortable shirt, and slip-on shoes.

In a moment I didn't expect, she closes the bedroom door to change clothes. Less than half an hour ago, she was ready to take off all her clothes and dance on my lap for twenty dollars. Now, modesty kicks in. It's nice to see that not everybody takes their work home with them.

After a minute, she emerges in the new outfit, and I'm struck once again by how pretty she is. Too late, I realize I'm staring, after she looks at me quizzically and asks, "What?"

"Nothing," I answer. "You're right. That outfit will work better." She accepts my answer. "Are you ready to go?"

"I think so. It's just ... I don't know how long I'll be gone. I mean, do I have to leave for a few days, a couple of weeks ... or am I running out on my lease?"

I sigh in sympathetic frustration. All very good questions. "I just don't know. This is the part I never stick around for. Until now, I've delivered the message and left the person to figure out the best course of action. The details that went with it weren't something I ever let myself think about."

"Well, maybe you should, Tristan. You march into people's lives uninvited, and you ... you, what? You give them this ... proclamation. And then you're out of there. See ya. Good luck with that whole re-arranging your life thing. Well, there's details. Jobs and apartments and family members and friends. And I sure as hell wish that message of yours came with a little bit of help about what to do about them."

The last part of her sentence trails off to quietness, as the tears she was fighting emerge. It isn't an all-out sob, more of an exhausted cry, coupled with the embarrassment of breaking down in front of a stranger.

I'm without a sense of what to do. Do I put my arms around her and hold her while she cries? Do I say the right thing, whatever the hell that is? Do I leave the room, to let her cry in private? I'm no good at these decisions. So mostly I stand there.

"I'm sorry," I say quietly. "I didn't mean to make you … you know."

"It's not your fault," she answers, then thinks a moment. "Well, it is, but it isn't. I'm just so tired, and all I wanted to do when I got home tonight was wash my hair and see what was on TV."

"I wish you could. I wish *I* could."

"What?" she says. "Wash your hair and watch TV?"

I laugh a little. "Yeah. Sounds a lot better than the way I spend most of my nights."

She laughs a bit too at the mental picture, and it's enough to stop her tears. She then walks over to me and runs the fingers of her right hand through my hair. The feeling is indescribable. It's human contact, unsolicited, unpurchased, and perfect. "Feels pretty clean to me," she comments.

"I do manage," I tell her. "On a good day, I'll even use conditioner."

"I can tell," she says, her tone relaxing at last. "I bet you're one of those lather-rinse-repeat kind of guys."

"Of course. It doesn't work if you don't repeat."

In spite of herself, she laughs at my corny joke. It's the closest I've felt to her yet, far closer than I felt when her naked body was inches from my face at that club. "So …" I offer. "Truce?"

"Truce," she says quietly.

"Thank you."

"Come on, let's go," she says. "I'm hungry."

Despite the pervasive hunger we both feel, we decide that a few miles' distance between ourselves and Key West is a good idea. So we get on U.S. 1 and head north into the night. I'm gently apprehensive as we pass through the key deer wildlife refuge. If my earlier conversation partner makes another appearance, Rebecca will probably lose it, and I'll be right on her heels. Fortunately, we traverse those miles with no sign of the chatty beast or any of his kin. *Suits me. Little know-it-all.* I've got no plans to fall in love with Rebecca Traeger, no matter how beautiful, sensitive, intelligent, and strong she seems.

We hold out for a full hour, arriving in Marathon, halfway back to Miami. There's an all-night diner there, so we park and go inside, taking a booth in the corner. There are a couple of locals at the counter, more interested in politics than food, and a weary-looking young couple at a table across the room, appearing less than delighted with what they've been served. I tell myself that I'm not scoping out the place, looking for potential threats. Then I remember that I probably wouldn't know a potential threat if it kneed me in the balls and asked, "You the guy lookin' for potential threats?" So I suppress any notions of myself as private investigator or bodyguard or anything even vaguely heroic, and consign myself to the role of chauffeur.

I order a club sandwich with mashed potatoes, and she gets pancakes with link sausage. It's close to midnight, not a time I traditionally associate with breakfast, but I have to admit that her pancakes look awfully good. It never fails; anytime I go to a restaurant with another person, whatever they order always looks much better than whatever I order. That's probably why most of the time, I eat alone.

Halfway through the meal, she breaks the silence. "Are we gonna drive through the night?"

"I don't know," I reply. "I hadn't thought that far ahead yet. I suppose we could."

"I can split the driving with you," she offers.

I disagree. "I'm the only authorized driver on the account. They don't have a copy of your license, so you can't drive the rental car."

She shrugs dismissively. "It's not like they can see us. That only matters if there's an accident or something. And if that happens, we can just switch drivers before the cops show up."

"And if we're dismembered and unconscious at the scene?"

"Then who's on the rental car agreement is the least of our worries, isn't it?" she replies with a self-satisfied little smile.

Before I can retort, the front door to the diner opens, and a man of about sixty enters. I hate to sound classist, but *shabby-looking* is the word that comes to mind when I see him. He may be a fine human being and a good family man, but to my tired and cautious eyes, he looks shabby. I watch as he scans the room, looking at the few patrons keenly. Seeing us, he begins to approach. Rebecca's back is to him, but there's no mistaking the look on my face, and she quickly turns to see him draw near.

"Stay calm," I say to her discreetly. I see her reach for something in her pocket. Some kind of weapon, I can only surmise, though specifically what, I can't tell.

I try to take my own advice and not panic as he walks right up to our table. Unfortunately, my extrasensory abilities aren't something I can switch on and off, allowing me to look at this man and know what he's about to do. The only way I'll know what he's going to do is when I see him do it.

I don't have to wait long. Without hesitation, he speaks to us. "I'm sorry to bother you," he says in a voice that bespeaks a life of deprivation, "but I'm hungry and I have no money. Do you have any change, so I could buy a meal?"

Behind the counter, the manager on duty calls out before I can answer. "I've asked you not to bother my customers!"

He turns to the counterman. "I'm sorry, Andrew. It's late and there's no one outside to ask …"

"It's all right," I tell him, finding ten dollars in my pocket and handing it to him. A look of surprise and relief spreads over his face. His entreaty, I suspect, is too often met with rejection at best, outright hostility more often.

"Oh, thank you!" he says sincerely. "I'm going to sit down right over there and buy some food. I promise I won't buy booze or cigarettes or anything like that." I believe him; he smells of neither of those things. "God bless you, sir," he says. "Don't fall in love."

The moment freezes in my mind. Though I can't see it, I'm sure my expression must be priceless. *No, it's not possible.* "I'm sorry, what did you say?"

"I said I can't thank you enough."

"Oh." I look at Rebecca, and her face suggests that his words of thanks are what she heard too. "You're welcome. Enjoy your food."

He makes his way over to the counter, and I'm peripherally aware of him presenting himself to the contentious employee as a legitimate customer and receiving only the most requisite and begrudging courtesy in return. I realize that in the eyes of my traveling companion, I still look frozen like a … well, I won't use the expected simile of forest animals and headlights.

"What's with that face?" she asks. It's a fair question.

"Nothing. I just … I didn't know what he wanted, that's all."

"No," she points out. "When you didn't know what he wanted, you looked calm and in control of the moment. After you *did* know what he wanted, you got the vaguely catatonic look on your face."

Damn her observational skills.

"It's …" I start, remaining stone-faced. "It's just that …"

"What?"

"That man is my father. I haven't seen him in over twenty years."

She looks at me, astonished. "Oh my God … you're shitting me."

"Of course I'm shitting you. Now shut up and eat your pancakes before I decide that they look better than what I'm having."

She throws an orange slice at my head and tries unsuccessfully not to laugh. "You know, part of getting me to trust you includes not making up weird shit on our first date."

The word catches me off guard. "This is a date?"

"Might as well be," she says, finishing a pancake. "You're buying breakfast."

With the food consumed and the bill paid (by me; she wasn't kidding), we exit the eatery and find ourselves back in the parking lot. Only a few cars travel the highway at this hour. We stand there for about thirty seconds, absently watching the traffic go by. "Were you scared?" she asks.

"I don't know. Maybe a little. When he came over to the table, you reached for something in your pocket. Can I ask what it is?"

She pulls out a canister of pepper spray. "I'm not afraid to use it," she says. Though the words are informational in nature, I can't help feeling there's an implied threat in them, should the circumstance warrant it.

"Good to know," I answer unemotionally.

Again we stand in silence, watching as a semi truck and three more cars head up U.S. 1.

"Tristan?"

"Yeah?"

"I was wrong. I don't think I can drive through the night. I'm pretty tired."

"Yeah, me too."

"Can we get a room here in … Where are we again?"

"Marathon," I reply. "I think that's a pretty good idea."

Within five minutes, we are at the Days Inn, standing at the registration desk, blearily facing a desk clerk who possesses the nocturnal alertness that comes with working third shift. "We'd like two rooms for one night," I say to him.

"Can't help you there," he replies, earning a confused look from me.

"But your sign said 'vacancy.'"

"Yep," he says, "but if you'll notice, it don't say vacan*cies*. All I got's one room."

He has no reason to lie, yet I find it hard to believe. "In Marathon, Florida at one in the morning on a Thursday night?"

He gives a little laugh. "You must not be from around here." There's a snide retort in me, but I resist. "It's Pelican Days!" he continues proudly.

"It's what?" Rebecca says. She's a lot closer to a native than I am, and the term means nothing to her either.

"Pelican Days," he repeats. "Four-day festival of fishing, boating, and beach parties. Every place in town is booked solid until Monday. Heck, only reason I've got the one room is because I had a last-minute cancellation by a fella from Atlanta."

"We can keep driving," I suggest to Rebecca.

"No," she says, "I'm so tired." She turns to the clerk. "Does the room have two beds?"

"Two queens," he says. He then gives us a scrutinizing eye. "You two married?"

"Engaged," I say flatly, "but passionately in love. Can we have the room?"

"Well, normally during Pelican Days, our minimum rental is two nights, but you two look pretty worn out, and I'd hate to be the cause of a car crash because I turned you away. I can let you have it for the one night."

"Thank you," Rebecca says, relieved.

"Fill this out," he says, sliding me a registration form and a pen. "It'll be eighty-nine fifty plus tax."

My credit card is in his hand without my even remembering extricating it from my wallet. Within two minutes, the charge is approved, the form is completed, and an actual metal room key is in my hand. I haven't seen one in years.

"Room 116," the clerk says. "You go out this door, park around the back. You'll have an ocean view, come morning. Breakfast is from six to nine in the room right off the lobby."

"Thanks," I say to him. I can feel the fatigue taking over, along with the relieved feeling that the day's activities are over and I can actually let myself sleep.

"You two get some rest," the man says with genuine concern in his voice. "You look like the devil himself's been chasin' you."

I manage a weak smile. "Let's hope not, anyway."

Chapter 4

Room 116 of the Marathon Days Inn is unlikely to earn any praise from the Michelin Guide, but it is clean, quiet, and very inviting to our weary eyes. Rebecca brings in one of her suitcases, and I bring in the travel bag I've had with me in the Sebring's trunk. A quick visual inspection of the room tells us all we need to know. The two queen beds are there, as promised, neatly made up, and—barring close inspection under a black light, anyway—clean enough to sleep in.

"You can use the bathroom first if you want to," I tell her.

"Thanks." She takes a toiletry kit from her bag and starts in that direction, but then hesitates outside the bathroom door. "It …" She searches for the right words. "I'm sure I don't have to say this, but … nothing's gonna happen tonight."

Is she seeing the future now? "Huh?"

"With us, I mean. Nothing's gonna …"

Got it now. "Oh, right, of course. I wouldn't."

"That's not to say …"

"You don't have to …" I tell her.

"I just don't know you …"

The question comes out before I can stop it. "Does that mean if you *did* know me, that …"

"What?"

"Nothing. Stupid question. I … recant. I …"

"Retract?" she offers.

"Right. I un-ask what I just asked."

"Please tell me that isn't what this is about," she says, disappointment lacing her tone.

"No, no, I ... it was a stupid question and I don't know where it came from. This is about sleep, and if there were two rooms available, I would have paid for two rooms. Honestly. I'm very tired, and I didn't know about Pelican Days or whatever the hell it's called. Look, if you want, I can sleep in the car."

"You can't sleep in the car."

"There's room in the back seat."

"Tristan ..."

"Because I don't want to make ..."

"*Tristan.*"

I am rambling and I know it. The unique kind of rambling that happens after you say something you wish you hadn't said, and you figure that if you add enough words on *any* topic, the unfortunate words on *that* topic will be buried and gone and forgotten about. Not this time. The elephant not only entered the room, it took a mighty shit on the bed. Now my honor and my intentions are in question, and despite her sincere-sounding utterance of the words, "It's all right. I'm sorry I brought it up," the remainder of the trip is in danger of smelling like elephant.

"Okay," I reply. "Sorry."

She goes into the bathroom and closes the door, and I'm left alone in the room to bang my head against the wall, if I were the type of person who would bang his head against the wall in situations such as this one. Fortunately for head, wall, and the occupants of room 117, I am not that person.

Do I even want her that way? I suppose I'm biologically programmed to think so. Pretty young woman, available man. Pass on my DNA, continue the species; high school biology at its finest. But I don't want to marry this girl, and my DNA is the last thing on my mind. I have a long trip ahead with Rebecca, and I have to know if I can control any feelings I have for her. I mean, we've just met, so there's no deep emotional attachment. Anything I feel would strictly be—for lack of a more sophisticated expression—dick-related. It's been so long since I've felt human contact that transcended the delivery of a message.

But shit, she needs to be able to trust me. And more importantly, *I* need to be able to trust me. Otherwise, the road to Ohio is going to be littered with uncomfortable silences, physical and emotional distances between us, and me apologizing for my feelings over and over again. To hell with it. The deer was right—don't fall in love, which at the moment includes "don't give in to lust."

And then she comes out of the bathroom in a long white shirt and a pair of shorts that she's planning to sleep in. Were this an old Tex Avery cartoon, I suspect my tongue would be depicted as four feet long, unfurling onto the floor. My eyes would be on springs, my heart likewise, accompanied by an absurdly exaggerated pounding sound. And to cap it off, I'd be making a wolf whistle at the sight of her. Tex Avery understood the male of the species.

"It's all yours," she says to me, and for the moment, I'm so distracted that I don't even understand what she's referring to.

"What?" I ask, rapidly and silently praying to myself that she's referring to her body.

"The bathroom," she replies, with just enough of an old-school *duh* undertone to make me feel stupid for asking. "I'm done in there."

"Oh. Right."

"Be careful. The floor's a little wet."

I get up and make my way toward the bathroom. Before I can close the door, she says, "Tristan, I'm sorry about what I said earlier. I'm sorry I assumed the worst about you."

This is it, the opportunity to be noble, to be the bigger person and own up to my part in making her feel that way in the first place. Instead, I hear myself uttering in a mock-wounded tone, "I just hope you understand that's not how I am."

Nice. Mature. Asshole.

Even in the depths of sleep, I am aware of intense, searing pain. Without an organ or a body part to call home, it seems to reside in my very soul. It sounds melodramatic, but that's the only way I can describe it. Imagine your least favorite headache, back pain, stomach ache, or stubbed toe. Agonizing as it is, it has a home, and the rest of your body is sheltered from it. And if you're very lucky, there are pills in the medicine cabinet that will take it away. The pain I am experiencing now has no place of residence; it simply fills me, like it has so many times before, and no pill will relieve it.

Through the pain, I remember that Rebecca is in the room, and I try not to cry out and wake her. Freaking her out will do nothing to improve our already shaky relationship. So I try to rationalize and focus on my breathing and wait for the inevitable words that follow the hurt—the mental telegram that tells me where my life will go next.

Right on schedule, it arrives. Words; pictures to accompany them. *Tarpon Springs, Florida.* In my mind, I see a small coastal village. Fishing boats line a pier. *Stelios Papathanissou.* A man's face comes to mind, his body shortly thereafter. He is dressed in what looks like a space suit. The image is confusing. NASA is in Cape Canaveral, not Tarpon Springs. Details come into focus. A trident, a breathing apparatus. It's a diving suit, not a space suit. This man is a fisherman.

One by one, the details arrive—where to go, what to tell him. Then, as if I were contemplating not doing it, the message ends with a particularly heinous streak of pain that runs through me. Diligently as I have been trying to remain quiet, it is too much, and I sit up with a shout.

This startles and scares Rebecca enough to rouse her from sound sleep, and she emits a shriek. I turn on the light by the bedside. My eyes are now focused enough to see the clock. It's almost 6 AM.

"What is it?" she asks, a bit panicked. "What's wrong?"

"I'm sorry," I say wearily, the pain starting to subside now. "I'm sorry. I tried to be quiet. I got another ... assignment."

She's confused. How could she not be? Seconds ago, she was sleeping peacefully. Now she's bolted awake by my voice. "Assignment? Did someone call?"

"No. It's not like that. I just ... got the details of the next message I have to deliver. You know, in my head."

She takes a moment to try to wrap her mind around this. The only question that comes to her is, "What time is it?"

"Five fifty-two," I answer.

"Shit," she says quietly. "Does this mean we have to get up? Does this mean we have to leave now?"

"No, no. It's not like that. You can go back to bed for a bit. I won't be able to sleep again, but I'll sit quietly in bed and let you sleep."

I suspect that adrenaline has her too wound up to fall asleep again now. "So … that was it? That was what happens when you get one of these … message things?"

"That was a quieter version," I say to her. "Out of respect for you, I internalized a lot of the screaming."

"Jesus, how do you stand it?"

"I'm not sure."

"But wait a second," she says. "How can you start another one when you're still working on mine?"

"Sometimes I have to multitask. Besides, whatever it is that wants me to do this didn't count on you still being with me. It's okay. We can make this work. It'll just be a short detour, and it won't really out of our way."

"So … where are we going?"

"Tarpon Springs. North and west of here. Over by Tampa."

"What's there?"

"A fisherman. Apparently, if I don't talk to him before 3:00 this afternoon, he's going to have a very bad day."

She looks at me in amazement. "My God … this is real. This is really real."

I'm surprised by her reaction. "You mean after everything we've already been through together, you still had your doubts?"

"I … I don't know. I guess I believed you enough to quit my job and come with you. But this just makes it—more real, I suppose." There is a moment of silence between us. "Can I get you something … for the pain, I mean?"

"Thanks, but no. It'll be with me until we head out and I'm moving in the direction of Tarpon Springs. Once it's convinced I'm going to deliver the message, it won't hurt anymore."

"Then we should go," she says, getting out of bed.

"No, you should get some more sleep."

"It's okay. I got a few hours. That's enough. If leaving here now makes you stop hurting, that's more important."

Now it's my turn to offer a surprised look in her direction. "You really care about whether or not I'm in pain. Why?"

She appears embarrassed by the question, as if her display of human compassion is akin to some sort of confession. "I don't know. I just do.

31

I guess I want to think of you as a friend, since we're in this together. Maybe I think you're kind."

"Kind?" The word sounds almost archaic in the air, having fallen so far out of use in today's don't-give-a-shit society. I like it, and I want to embrace it as a personal trait, but I have to wonder. "Looking back at last night, do you really think I've earned such a compliment?"

"Well, yes, you did come into my workplace, disrupt my life, and make me quit my job. And you've said some things that were hard to hear. But when you look at me, it's like I can see your thoughts about me."

Holy shit, I hope she can't see all of them.

"You look at me like you want me to live and be safe. Like you think of me as a person. I see so many men every day, and they see right through me. Most of them look at me like I exist only at the level of my chest and between my legs. The rest look at me as if I'm going to fall in love with them and run away together, just because they handed me a dollar bill and I paid attention to them for thirty seconds. With interactions like that, do you wonder why I'm not in a relationship?"

"No, I guess not." I'm curious about something, so I ask her. "Do you hate all men because of that?"

"No," she answers matter-of-factly. "At first, when I started dancing, I wanted to hate them. But I realized it's the nature of the business relationship. When you walk into Burger King and hand them money, you expect them to be friendly to you and hand you a burger and fries. If you spend a little more, you might treat yourself and get a milkshake. When men walk into the club and hand me money, they expect to see my naked body, and have me be friendly to them. And if they spend a little more, they treat themselves to a table dance. It's a business transaction, and I can't hate them for making it."

"You might mention that to Fantasia," I reply. "I think she was trying to suffocate me with her breasts."

"Fantasia's got issues. She's rocking the angry lesbian thing, and she thinks that a good show makes up for shitty customer service."

I laugh a bit. "You're awfully lucid for six in the morning."

"You forget, I work nights. If it weren't for our little road trip tiring me out, I'd be in my prime right now. But I've had my nap and my philosophical discussion, so I'm ready to hit the road. I wouldn't say no to breakfast. I might even be persuaded to buy."

I stand up with a smile. "Well, hell, why didn't you say so? A sunrise drive through the Keys *and* a free breakfast? You've touched the heart of this world-weary old man."

"You're not old," she says.

"Oh yeah? Glad you think so."

"Come on. What are you, thirty?"

"Thirty-*six*," I correct her.

Her response is one of disbelief. "What? No way."

"Honest."

"Well … you don't look thirty-six."

"Thank you. In deference to my advanced years, do you mind if I use the bathroom first this morning?"

"Help yourself, Grandpa," she says with a wicked little smile.

"Hey, watch that shit," I warn her. "You're not too big to put over my knee."

"Ooh, baby," she jokes right back.

The banter feels good. It feels friendly and natural, like we've removed a wall between us and we can kid with each other this way. I know she was frightened of me at first, and I suppose I was frightened of her too. This trip is such a departure from the way every other message delivery has gone in the past. I'm afraid of screwing it up; of screwing *her* up. I know I have to be very careful with her, especially now that she's starting to trust me. There's a side of me that could easily and carelessly exploit that for my own personal gain. Wouldn't be the first time, either.

By 6:20, we are in the car and heading north again on U.S. 1. The sun is making its way over the eastern horizon, painting the waters of the Atlantic in orange, yellow, and pink. There isn't much traffic on the road, so I'm able to steal frequent glances to my right, to watch the show unfold. "What are you looking for?" Rebecca asks at one point.

"God," I answer flatly.

"Let me know if you find him," she says. "I've got some questions." And with that, she closes her eyes and tries to get some rest.

Within the hour, we are in Key Largo, and we stop at a local café that the residents favor. I indulge myself in a conch-and-tomato omelet. Conch—apart from the aesthetic qualities of its lovely and musical shell—is also damn tasty, and very hard to find outside of southern Florida and the Caribbean. So when I see it on the breakfast menu, of all places, it's hard to resist. It's a bit like calamari, but without the rubber band texture that ruins that dish for me.

It's reasonable to expect that by this point in the trip, Rebecca and I would have talked about ourselves in detail, and we would know each other rather well. But it isn't the case. I'm private by nature, and she is very hesitant to bring up any important subjects, such as family, work, school, or even details about her own life. Our travels are marked with long stretches of silence, which holds true as we eat our breakfast. So much so that when I ask, "How are your eggs?" after fifteen minutes without talking, she actually jumps a bit, startled to hear me speak.

"Huh? Oh, fine. How's your … fish thing?"

"My fish thing is lovely. Sure I can't talk you into some?"

"Uh, no. I never hit the seafood before noon."

"More for me," I reply. "I can't believe you've lived in Key West and never tried conch."

"I'm not big on fish," she says.

"It's shellfish." I cut a bit off and hold it up. "Here, just try it."

"No, *really*, it's okay. You look like you're into it, so you just go at it."

I shrug and continue eating. There is now a vacuum in the conversation, into which some words must be pulled. She provides them. "So how far are we from Tarpon Springs?"

"Once we get to Miami, about four hours."

"And from there, how long to Ohio?"

"Well, provided we don't get any more detours, about sixteen hours of driving."

"That feels like forever. Do you think we'll get more detours?"

"I honestly don't know. We might get none, we might get four."

She's not pleased with that answer. "And what if one of those detours wants you to go to … I don't know … California, just as we're getting ready to enter Ohio?"

I try to calm her fears. "Then California will wait until after I drop you off."

"But won't you be in terrible pain?"

"Maybe. We'll figure that out if it happens."

We finish breakfast and the waitress brings the check. As promised, Rebecca takes it and pays cash for the two meals. I notice that she leaves a generous tip as well. This makes sense, given the reliance on tips in her profession. Correction: her *former* profession.

Back on the road, we make decent time through the Miami metropolitan area before heading west on I-75 across the state. As the swampland sails past us on either side, conversation turns to questions.

"Is it a man?" she asks me.

"Yes."

"Is he alive?" she inquires further.

"Yes."

"Is he American?"

"Yes."

"Is he famous?"

"No, it's my neighbor Pete. Of course he's famous. It'd be a little difficult if he weren't, don't you think?"

"Fine, then do I get a do-over on that question?"

"No, and your question about getting a do-over counts as a question. You're up to five."

She clicks her tongue in annoyance, but doesn't argue my shady interpretation of the rules. "Is he a politician?"

"Geez, you ask a lot of questions."

"Very funny. Just answer. Is he a politician?"

"No."

"Is he an actor?"

"Yes," I answer with a poker face.

"Is he a TV actor?"

"Yes."

"Is he on TV *now?*"

I think about it. "Mmmmm, no."

"Is he over forty?"

"Yes."

"Is it ... Ron Howard?"

"Nope."

"Is it Don Johnson?"

"Nope."

"Is he over sixty?"

"Yes."

"Is it Johnny Carson?"

"No. Good guess, although technically, Johnny was more of a television personality than a true actor."

"Is it Andy Griffith?"

"No."

"Okay," she says, "I give up. Who is it?"

"Pernell Roberts," I answer victoriously.

She looks at me as if I've just uttered the name of the vice prefect of the planet Glanurax IV. "I have no idea who that is, Tristan."

"Come on ... Pernell Roberts. From *Bonanza*." She shrugs in a total absence of recognition. "He went on to play Trapper John, M.D."

"What, on *M*A*S*H*?"

"No no, that was Wayne Rogers. Pernell Roberts played an older version of him on his own eponymous program."

"Look, if you want me to believe you're not old, you need to stop bringing up figures from ancient history. And you need to stop using the word 'eponymous.'"

"Thing one, my young friend: the 1960s to 1980s are *not* 'ancient history.' Thing two: it's not my fault if your personal pop cultural database stretches back only as far as Justin Timberland ..."

"Lake," she corrects.

"And thing three: I never said I wasn't old. *You* said I wasn't old."

There is the tiniest hint of a pout on her face as she realizes that I might just be right. "Unspeakably amusing as this is, can we do something else?" she requests.

"Okay. How about twenty questions on a subject you know a little better: you?"

The suggestion makes her visibly uneasy. "Do we have to?"

"No, we don't have to. But I'd like to know more about you, if you're willing to tell me."

Though she doesn't look thrilled with the concept, she lets her guard down enough to ask, "What do you want to know?"

"Well, how long had you been working at the club in Key West?"

"Eight months. Before that, I was a secretary for over a year. It didn't pay enough, though. So one night, I'm at a bar with some friends, and one of them tells me she dances at the Breezes. I'm a little surprised, but I figure, hey, whatever makes her happy. Then she tells me how much she brings home in a typical week, and I think, holy shit, it would take me two months to make that much. So I spent about a week and a half arguing with myself over whether I could do it. And then I swallowed my pride and went in and auditioned. Two days later, I'm on the stage, finally utilizing the ballet lessons and gymnastics my parents paid for ten years ago."

I catch something on her face as the story ends. "You flinched a little at the end there, when you mentioned your parents. Does that mean something?"

"We're in a convertible. Something brushed my face. You don't have to read anything into it." She sounds very defensive.

"Okay. Then you won't mind if my next question is about them."

"Them? My parents?"

"Your parents. When I delivered the message, you said you thought one of them had sent you. But you asked about each individually. First your father, then your mother. Does that mean they're not still together?"

"You playing detective now?" she asks.

"No, I'm just a good listener. And what I hear is you dodging the question."

"I'm not dodging."

Outside the car, a pelican flies alongside, just a few feet above our heads. I spend a few seconds watching the bird swoop and soar while Rebecca decides whether she will actually open up to me on this obviously sensitive subject.

"They're not still together," she answers quietly. "They haven't been for six years now. They still live in Ohio, but in different cities."

"When's the last time you talked to them?"

"Shortly after I left school. The relationship had been strained for a while already, and when I dropped out, it did nothing to endear me to them."

"I'm gonna go out on a limb and guess that they don't know about your most recent job opportunity."

"No." Then quickly, "But I'm not ashamed of it. There's nothing to be ashamed of."

"I'm not passing judgment," I remind her. "Remember, I'm the one who's been unemployed all this time."

"I thought when you're rich, that makes you a 'gentleman of leisure.'"

I give her a look of mild annoyance. "Look at me. Do I look like I'm leisurely?"

"Not so much."

She does open up to me about the family history, the circumstances that drove them apart, and the tensions that grew over the years. The conversation, while strained, does effectively pass the time as we make our way north and west across the state of Florida. As we pull into the city of Tarpon Springs, it is a few minutes before noon, and once again, it is time for me to change the life of a complete stranger.

Chapter 5

I have never been to Tarpon Springs, Florida before, but courtesy of the forces that have summoned me there, I have a turn-by-turn map in my mind of where to go to find Mr. Stelios Papathanissou, and thank God, too, because I think I'd have a hell of a time spelling his name if I had to look him up in the phone book.

The city isn't large, only about 20,000 people or so from the looks of it. As I turn off of the main highway onto Dodecanese Avenue, I see that the city is awash in Greek influence. Restaurants, shops, and even the boats themselves all bear Greek names. And the boats are everywhere, hundreds of them at the marina.

Rebecca is looking from side to side, taking it all in. In a moment of practicality, she asks, "Do we have time for lunch before you meet this guy?"

"Don't you think we should do what we came here to do first?" I reply.

"Don't you know it's rude to answer a question with a question?" she retorts.

"Don't *you?*" I volley back.

"Amusing as this banter is," she says, "I'm hungry, and I thought you said we're fine if you talk to him before 3:00."

"We're fine if I *convince* him before 3:00," I answer. "Not everyone is as easily convinced as you. I want to find him, give him the message, and then see if I need to spend time with him to persuade him. Then we can eat."

"Fine," she says, "but if it's another three hours until lunch, I'm gonna be cranky."

"I seem to recall something about us not being partners. I can drop you off at any restaurant you like, and then come get you when I'm done."

"No …" she answers quickly, then regains her calm. "I want to watch you work … if that's all right."

I think about it for a moment; it's a new circumstance, one I've never had to deal with before. I don't imagine there are any rules prohibiting it, and from what I know of the details of the assignment, there's no inherent danger in it. I allow her to join me, and she looks clearly enthusiastic about the prospect of it.

"Let me do the talking," I caution.

"Hey, that's fine. I'm just along for the ride. So … where do we find this guy?"

"Slip 218," I reply, looking at the slip numbers as they climb sequentially.

"You nervous?" she asks.

I am, but I don't necessarily want her knowing that. "There's a certain level of anxiety as I approach each new assignment. You never know how people are going to react. Some are abusive, others are openly aggressive. Some even think they can come with me while I work."

"Ha ha," she says humorlessly. "I wonder who *that* could be."

I see the sign on my left for slips 210 to 219 and find a parking spot as close as I can to the marina. After putting the top up, I get out of the car, and Rebecca follows right behind. I scan the harbor, looking for 218. It is the fourth one out on the right-hand side, and parked at it is a thirty-foot fishing boat named *Calliope*. I'm certainly not an authority on fishing boats, so I can't state with any assurance that it's a lovely boat or it isn't. It's clearly seen many years of service, and its owner has not gone out of his way to keep it pristine. It bears the scars and blemishes of its trade, but by the same token, it's not about to sink to the bottom of the Gulf of Mexico.

Not for three hours, anyway.

As we approach the boat, I notice a lone man standing on its deck.

As always, we've never met, and as always, I recognize him instantly, courtesy of the message I've received. He is Stelios Papa … Papathan … the Greek guy who's in some serious trouble if he doesn't listen to what I have to say.

We stop right at the gangplank and I call out to him. "Hello?"

"Hello, yes?" he replies, turning to face us. "What can I do for you?"

He seems pleasant enough. I estimate he's approaching sixty years old. His hair and face and hands speak of a life of hard work and salt water, but his eyes have a pleasant air about them. He clearly loves his work, which will make what I have to tell him all the more difficult.

"Are you Stelios?" I ask, already knowing the answer.

"This is me," he replies amiably. "And who are you, my friend?"

"My name is Alex," I tell him, dismissing Rebecca's next retort with a discreet but insistent glance over my shoulder. "I have a message to give you."

"And who is your friend?" Stelios asks, clearly impressed by the sight of Rebecca.

Before I can answer, she introduces herself. "Persephone," she says.

He's impressed. But with her looks, she could have said "Dog Turd" and gotten the same enthusiastic reaction. "A beautiful name for a beautiful young lady. Please, come aboard my boat and we'll talk."

Knowing what I know, I am initially hesitant but decide it will help my case. We board and Stelios invites us to sit on benches on deck. He offers us a drink, but I politely decline on behalf of us both. It's go time; no more stalling. This is the part I hate, but there's no way around it and no easy way to launch into it. "Stelios, this will sound strange, and let me assure you that we don't mean you any harm. I know that you're planning to take your boat out on the water at 3:00 today, and I need to warn you that there's a problem with the starboard engine. If you take the boat out, the engine will catch fire, and there's likely to be a hull breach, which would cause your boat to sink. So please, before you go out again, take care of that engine. I'd hate to see anything happen to you."

I pause, looking at his face for any sign of a reaction. He remains curiously unaffected—much more so than anyone in recent memory.

I wait a few seconds for a response, expecting disbelief, but still he remains silent. I've done all I can; it's time to go.

"I'm sorry to bring you bad news like that," I say to him. "We'll go and let you see to your repairs."

As Rebecca and I walk toward the gangplank, Stelios breaks his silence. There is a curious tone to his voice—not anger, not confusion, but more … acceptance; confirmation. "That's all? You're just going to tell me this and walk away, Alex? Or should I say *Tristan?*"

The sound of my name stops me in my tracks. I shoot Rebecca a swift, accusing glance, and her expression instantly and clearly replies, *Hey, don't look at me.*

I turn around to face the fisherman again, and my eyes ask *How?* without my mouth saying a word. He nods a bit and gives a little chuckle, as he says, "You think you are the only one with *gifts?*" To emphasize, he taps a finger on the side of his head. "You're hungry," he says, informing us rather than asking us. "It's been a long drive for you to come here. I have moussaka ready in the galley, and I insist you stay and join me for lunch. Maybe we can answer some questions for each other."

The boat isn't elegant, but it feels like home, because for Stelios it is home. He spends more time here, he tells us, than he does at the small apartment he rents in Tarpon Springs. Over plates of moussaka—a wondrous dish made of ground lamb and eggplant, the best I've ever had, the first Rebecca has ever had—he describes a life spent fishing. Forty-three years of it. He started off as a sponge fisherman, then, when the industry fell on hard times, he switched to more traditional fishing. And when sponge fishing resumed in the Gulf, he was one of the first to jump back on the bandwagon. He is friendly and charming, a bit flirty toward Rebecca, and for the moment, he is avoiding the all-important questions.

At the risk of discourtesy, I steer the conversation. "I'm curious about your gifts," I tell him. "How you knew my name."

"I have the sight," he says simply. "God's third eye, my grandmother called it. I can see the truth in people. Sometimes I know what will happen before it happens."

"When I told you about the engine, you didn't seem surprised. Did you know there was a mechanical problem?"

"I suspected," he answers. "My sight told me to be careful, but I couldn't see what the exact trouble was. But my sight told me I would be safe. It must have known you were coming to warn me." He laughs. "Tristan's psychic boat repair, eh?"

"Let's say *boat diagnostics,*" I amend. "My gift doesn't come with repair skills, unfortunately."

"Oh, I can fix it," he says confidently. "It's the intake manifold. I will bet you money. So maybe I stay in dock today and don't go out. I lose a little income, but at least I don't go live with the sponges. I think they wouldn't be too happy with me, no?"

We laugh at the casual, easy way he has. It's so refreshing to be met with gratitude, rather than doubt, suspicion, and fear. Finally, someone else understands what it feels like to carry around thoughts that don't belong to you. But how much does he understand?

"Stelios …" I hesitate a moment, unsure of how to ask him. "Do you know why I've been chosen to do this? To tell people these things?"

He looks at me and thinks a moment. "For the same reason I am a fisherman. Because you can."

It's a logical answer, but it doesn't help me much. "Can you see how long I'll be asked to do this? Is there a time when I'll be able to stop?"

"I think you will do this until you can't do it anymore. Just like me with my boat. Someday, I won't be able to fish anymore. And thanks to you, that someday isn't today."

"But …" I search for the right words, still trying to understand. "Why send me at all? Things happen. Accidents occur. Sometimes people die. Why set that in motion and then send someone to keep it from happening?"

He nods; now my question is clear to him. A variation on the age-old selfish cry: *Why me?*

"You ever send a message you wish you could take back?" he asks simply. "A phone message, maybe an e-mail?"

"I guess so," I answer.

"Maybe God does too."

The answer is unexpectedly profound and metaphysical, coming from this ordinary man. Of course, that may be my unintentional classism surfacing, equating lack of an advanced degree with lack of wisdom and sophistication.

My silence leaves Rebecca an opening and she grabs it. "Stelios, I have a question too …"

He laughs at this. "I think you are confusing Greek with gypsy. I should be telling you to cross my palm with silver, maybe!" She looks confused by this.

"It's something gypsy fortune tellers said in old movies," I explain.

He invites her to continue. "Don't worry, little Persephone. You can ask me your question."

"Tristan told me I had to leave my job, leave Florida, and go back to Ohio. He told me it was for my own safety, but he couldn't see why I had to leave. Do you know why I have to leave? What the danger is?"

He looks at her intently from across the table without saying a word. He then reaches out and holds her hands in his for many seconds, still not giving an answer. I watch as he opens that third eye he spoke of and searches deep within Rebecca's very being, trying to complete the message I started—the *why* to my *what*.

Stelios stares at her for thirty seconds, then forty-five. Almost a full minute passes before he releases her hands and says, "No, I can't see it."

"You can't?" I ask, surprised.

"It … changes," he says cryptically. "Today's danger may be different tomorrow."

"What does that mean?" Rebecca asks.

"I wish I knew," Stelios says quietly. "Sometimes, what I see is very clear to me. Other times, it's like I'm seeing it through cloudy water. You, my little Persephone, are very cloudy water. Maybe you stay with Stelios for a few days, the image will get clearer."

She smiles pleasantly, looking for the right words to decline, but I beat her to the punch. "Tempting as that is, we have to head north. Your moussaka and your hospitality were impeccable, though. And thank you for sharing what you shared with me."

We all rise, and Rebecca is the first to the gangplank. She makes her way back to the pier, and I am about to follow her, when I feel a hand on my shoulder. Stelios pulls me aside to speak to me privately.

"You know, don't you, that you can't fall in love with this girl?" he says discreetly.

I notice that Rebecca is watching us from the dock, but she can't hear what we're saying.

"So I've been told," I answer quietly. "But no one can tell me why."

"The water is not as cloudy as I let her think. But she can't know the reasons, not now."

The question I've been pondering and dreading surfaces, because I know that he may be the only one who can answer it for me. "Stelios … am I the danger she has to avoid?"

"Tristan?" she calls to me from shore. "You coming?"

"Be right there," I call back, then look back at the fisherman.

"You might be. But you must take her where she needs to go. She needs you. And you need her."

"I need *her*?"

"You will. Soon. Now go on. There's a long way to travel yet."

"Thank you, Stelios."

"Be careful, Tristan."

I rejoin Rebecca on dry land as Stelios goes to get his toolkit. "What were you two talking about?" she asks me.

"You know, boy stuff. Football, beer, pretty girls."

"I see. Was one of those girls me?" she asks coyly.

"Come on, you know I can't violate the sanctity of boy stuff."

We make our way back to the car, climb inside, and lower the top again. The weather is pleasant today, not too hot. Good driving weather, which is a good thing, since there's a hell of a lot of that to do.

As we pull out of Tarpon Springs, Rebecca asks me, "So, did we just save that man's life?"

I smile a little at the realization that she's right. "Yeah, I think we did."

"God, that's freaky. And how weird was that when he called you by your name? I saw you look at me like 'what did you tell him?' But then you knew I didn't tell him anything."

"It was a little disconcerting, I have to admit."

"Think how I feel!" she says. "Two days ago, I thought that psychics were just people trying to scam you out of twenty bucks in a storefront. Then I meet you *and* Stelios, and all of a sudden it's like a psychic fair."

I don't respond, and the absence of a reply affects her. "What?" she says. "What is it?"

I feel caught. "Nothing. It's nothing."

"It doesn't look like nothing. Did he say something to you? What did he tell you?"

"Rebecca, it's nothing, really."

"He told you what's going to happen to me, didn't he?" she guesses. "He couldn't tell me, but he told you ..."

"No," I reply quickly, and for the most part honestly. "He doesn't know and I don't know."

"If you do know, I want you to tell me. Even if it's bad, I want to know. Promise me you'll tell?"

"I promise."

A familiar silence ensues for about ten minutes, but I start to feel guilty because of it, so I start up the conversation again. "So when did you change your name?"

The question catches her off guard. "What are you talking about?"

"At some time, you must have changed your name to Rebecca. I was just wondering when. And, you know ... why."

"Why do you think I changed my name?"

"I didn't until today. When we boarded that boat, I told Stelios my name was Alex. I usually give a false name, to avoid complications. You decided to play along and you told him your name was Persephone. But when he saw through me, he started calling me Tristan. And to the end, he called you Persephone. So I have to think that it's your real name, which is why he didn't see through it."

I can see her working it out inside, considering whether she can make something up to cover for it, and then deciding that the truth is out. "On my eighteenth birthday. I was tired of my old name. And Rebecca was my middle name anyway, so I changed it legally."

"You were tired of your old name. That's the only reason?"

"Yes. Why?"

She sounds defensive, and I don't want to upset her. "Well, it's just that a legal name change is a big step. Most people who don't like their name just go by a nickname unofficially. I just wondered if there was something more that was motivating it. Some reason why Persephone wouldn't want to be Persephone anymore?"

She is silent, and I can't tell why. Either I've offended her by asking because she was telling the truth or I've upset her by asking because there's something more she isn't telling me. Whichever the case, I won't get anything else by prying, so I do the honorable thing … for a change.

"I'm sorry. It's none of my business."

The apology seems to disarm her a bit. "It's okay. I shouldn't have snapped at you. We're gonna be in this car together for a long time, and I should be friendlier. You want to know more about me; that's natural. It's just …"

"Just?" I prompt.

"What happens once we get to Ohio? After you drop me off? Are we going to be friends? Will we call each other? Send e-mails? Christmas cards? Or will you just drop me off and never see me again?"

"I don't know," I tell her. "I hadn't thought about it. This is all new terrain for me."

"Because …" she starts, "I feel like this is a big thing we're going through together. You may have even saved my life, I don't know. And I feel like that should make us … you know … *friends*. But that takes an investment of myself. And I'm not sure I'm ready to invest that, because I just don't know where I stand with you, Tristan."

She has me dead to rights, and I have no defense. "Nobody does, Rebecca. You want to know the real me? That's the real me. A man who's been unable to have a meaningful relationship with anyone in years. Even before this whole crazy mission of mine started. Maybe that's why I was chosen—somebody knew I wouldn't be leaving anybody behind. You know the reason why I let you come along with me? Do you think it was because I was being nice? No. It's because for a couple of days, I had the chance to interact with someone on a personal level. Someone pleasant. Someone … pretty. And now it seems that I couldn't even do *that* right. Because you're sitting there, and you don't know what to make of me, just like the rest of the world."

In my peripheral vision, I see that she is looking intently at me as I look at the road ahead. I feel naked in front of the former stripper, and with each second that passes without a word spoken by Rebecca, I feel smaller and smaller. If she rejects me now, after opening myself up to her this way, I'm fairly certain I'll vanish into a diminishing puddle of my own self-doubt.

Just before that moment arrives, I hear her quietly utter: "I want to be your friend."

My difficult brain tries to invent other things I might have misheard her say, but I realize at once how unhelpful that is, and I am willing to accept that she may have actually said what I thought she said.

Gracious, thoughtful people would respond, "Thank you." I respond, "Why?"

"Because you're unexpected," she replies directly. *Curious response.*

"Unexpected like a bee sting?" I ask.

"No, unexpected like a warm day in December, when you're sick and tired of the cold. *That's* what you are. You're that warm day."

"I have no people skills," I say apologetically. "I haven't since this whole thing began two years ago. Now I travel around so much, and the nature of what I do is so isolating …"

"You have no people skills because you have no people. Now you have a person. And I promise, when you act like a dick, I'll gently let you know, so you can work on those skills."

A surprising amount of happiness is starting to well up inside of me. And I swear that I am on the verge of smiling broadly and saying something very kind and thoughtful to her. Unfortunately, at this precise moment, the universe chooses to fuck me once again.

A wave of intense pain starts at the base of my spine and rockets up into my neck and my head. This is new, this is unique; I've never before gotten a message while I was behind the wheel of a car. My vision blurs, and my hands clutch the steering wheel so tightly, small rips appear in the vinyl under my fingernails.

I am marginally aware that drivers around me are honking and swerving, trying to get out of my way as I try to get out of theirs. The message is coming in, loud, persistent, fast, detailed. But I can't crash the car. I think Rebecca is calling my name. When I don't respond, I feel her grip the wheel and pull us to the shoulder of Route 19. As the message plays out and the pain subsides, I feel the presence of mind to take my foot off the gas pedal and move it to the brake. Once we come to a complete stop, I put the Sebring in park, and sit there for a moment, gasping for breath.

"So," she says calmly, "where are we going this time?"

I look at her, taken by her aplomb, while simultaneously terrified at how close I just came to crashing the car, and utter a single word: "Atlanta."

Chapter 6

A few minutes later, I am able to continue. Rebecca decides that safety is more important than the rental company's rules, so she takes the wheel as I rest up in the passenger's seat.

"So are you all right?" she asks as we continue north on Route 19. "Because that looked … shit, that looked pretty weird."

"You seemed calm at the time."

"I figure one of us had to be. Inside, I was scared. I didn't know if you were gonna be able to keep control of the car. You didn't tell me this could happen when you were driving."

"It never has before," I tell her.

"So why now?"

"Urgency, I think. We don't have much time to get there."

"Atlanta?" she says.

"Atlanta."

"What's the assignment?"

I give her the details and she looks anxious. I'm feeling it too this time. If I'm right, there's an awful lot at stake. "We have a little less than eight hours, and it'll take almost that long to get there," I inform her. "I want you to go no more than five over the speed limit."

"I can go twenty over if it'll help."

"It won't help us if we get pulled over. Keep it at five over and we should be fine."

"It's weird," she says, "it's just weird. This is so last-minute. I mean, as important as this is, you'd think they'd give you more time … whoever the hell *they* are."

"The best I can figure, this situation just arose, and there wasn't time to give me more warning." I shake my head as my strength slowly returns to me. "Something feels wrong about this. I know this sounds crazy, but something just feels … different, and not in a good way."

"You've never done one like this before?"

"Not exactly like this, no. Here, you'll want to get on I-75 North here."

She takes the on-ramp to the interstate, and we quickly accelerate to seventy-five miles per hour. Finding the words, she poses a difficult question. "What happens to you … if you can't help this person?"

"As long as I try, nothing bad will happen to me. I can't control whether they listen to my warning or not. If I refused to try … well, let's just say it wouldn't end well for me."

"Shit," she says quietly.

"Still want to be my friend?" I ask with a little laugh.

Her answer is sincere and without hesitation. "Yes. Of course I do." She almost sounds offended that I'd ask. "This is … Jesus, this is unique. Who else gets this opportunity? You're the only one, right?"

"I don't know. I've never met anyone else who does this, but there could be others. I just don't know."

"I've never read about anyone doing this," she says. "Never saw anybody on TV. This is such an amazing thing you do. Why don't you tell the world about this?"

"Rebecca, this is the age of reality television. The last thing I need for credibility is a camera crew following me around everywhere I go."

"Yeah, okay, I can see that." A realization comes to her. "Does that mean I'm the only person you've trusted with this?"

"Well, I have to give some detail to each person who gets a message, but you know more about it than anyone else."

"Does that make me your best friend?" she asks cheekily.

"When you grabbed the steering wheel, did you keep me from plowing into oncoming traffic and killing us both?"

"Well … yeah, I guess so."

"Then *that* makes you my best friend," I answer.

The hours of the afternoon speed by with the traffic on Interstate 75, as we make our way north from Florida into Georgia. After three uneventful hours with Rebecca behind the wheel, I feel well enough to resume the driving, so I thank her for the reprieve and take my traditional spot.

We make excellent time, though it is at the cost of anything remotely resembling sightseeing. Several times, Rebecca sees roadside signs advertising Florida's fun-filled attractions, and the look on her face must be a perfect replica of ones she displayed as a child on a family car trip, when Mom and Dad wouldn't stop at Circus World or Cedar Point.

Mom and Dad. Not a subject I'm likely to bring up in any hurry, since the mere mention of the pair yields instant introversion from my traveling companion. I don't want to think the worst, but years of being me make me wonder if there are skeletons in the closet, mental demons that drove Persephone Traeger as far from her identity and her home as possible.

She rouses me from my thoughts. "Do you have a nickname?"

"A nickname?" I repeat.

"Yeah. I mean Tristan is kind of a mouthful."

"This coming from Persephone?" I snicker.

"Which is why I went by Rebecca," she reminds me. "But I'm asking about *you* at the moment. So ... nickname?"

I think back on a life known more for solitude than socializing. "No, not really."

"Not even a shorter version of your name? Tris, or maybe Stan?"

"Do I look like a Stan?"

"No, not really. You look like Tristan. It's such an unusual name."

"It's Celtic," I explain. "One of the knights of the Round Table. Tragic hero and all that."

She smiles. "That fits you. Knight errant, rescuing the damsel in distress."

"That would be you, I'm assuming?"

"Naturally. So then your parents were big literature buffs, and you were named after this noble and tragic figure?"

"Oh, I wish. The real story is even more tragic. Back in those days, there was a brand of Irish whiskey called Tristan O'Mara. Mom was a big fan. And *that's* where my name comes from. Opinions are divided on whether her love of the beverage continued into her pregnancy, but let's just say it wouldn't surprise me."

"Shit," she replies in an apologetic tone.

"So, whatever you may feel about *your* parents, I'm guessing it's a safe bet you weren't named after booze."

"You should meet my brothers," she answers. "Muscatel and Thunderbird."

"You are such a little liar," I tell her, hiding my amusement.

"Is that any way to talk to your best friend?"

I have to laugh at that one. "No, I suppose it isn't."

We're both silent for several seconds before she decides to ask me, "Are we going to be safe? What you told me about this assignment … it sounds dangerous. Will we be all right?"

"There won't be a *we*. I want you to drop me off and be far away from there. This could go very wrong, and if it does, I don't want you anywhere near it."

"I can't just leave you there by yourself …"

"You forget: Before today, I did every one of these by myself."

"Yeah, but you told me you've never done one quite like this."

She argues well, I'll give her that.

"Rebecca … it's very thoughtful of you to want to help me. Maybe even noble, I'm not sure. But the very real truth is, what I'm doing tonight is extremely dangerous, and I could never live with myself if anything happened to you."

"I can take care of myself, Tristan. I've been doing it for years."

I think back to Stelios's warning—I might be the danger that Rebecca has to avoid. But then I remember his other warning: *She needs you. And you need her … You will. Soon.*

Could Rebecca be the key to my surviving this assignment? Stelios seemed sure, and there is certainly no dissuading her from wanting to join me.

"You can come with me," I tell her, and before her reaction can escalate to full childlike glee, I tack on the conditions. "But I want you at a safe distance. I don't want you by my side for this one. Five hundred feet away at least. Maybe more."

"Okay," she says, "but close enough that I can come help you if you call."

"All right. Just, please don't do anything risky. I know this all sounds very adventurous, but you have to believe me that I would give anything for this to be my last one. Never to have to do this again."

She absorbs the significance of that in silence. Maybe she has been romanticizing it a bit. And why not? On the surface it sounds glamorous and exciting, rushing in at the last moment to save people from a horrible fate. It's an honor. Maybe I should feel honored, but I don't. The first three or four times it happened, it was incredibly exhilarating. After that, it became a chore, then a duty, then a burden. It's well on its way to curse. And tonight it may very well be the death of me. Thinking about it, maybe I shouldn't be so quick to wish for this to be my last assignment. If it goes the way I think it will, that might just be the case.

It's a unique feeling, thinking that you may not live to see the next day. As I make my way north to Atlanta, the thought is very much on my mind, and it is not pleasant. It might be different if you've been suffering from a horrible, painful disease for years, but when you're relatively young and in good health, the possibility of not seeing tomorrow's breakfast is laced with dread.

The mind tries to temper the feeling by going over your life so far, pointing out all the good things you've done and the lives you've touched. But the thought of impending death keeps sneaking in, to undercut those achievements and taunt you with its …

"What are you thinking?" Rebecca asks.

For the record, I hate it when people ask me what I'm thinking. If I wanted them to know what I was thinking, I would be speaking instead. But the day has had some tense moments already, and this is no time to be unpleasant, so I simply say, "Nothing important," though it couldn't be further from the truth.

Actually, Rebecca, I'm thinking that there's a better than 50 percent chance that I'm going to be killed horribly tonight, and if I'm supremely unlucky, you will be too. On top of that, even if I do live to see tomorrow, I'm on a cross-country road trip with a woman who makes me feel uneasy, because I'm used to being alone. And I kind of like being alone, but now that you're here, I realize how desperate and pathetic I feel for wanting to be alone, because you're smart and friendly, and oh yeah, beautiful and young. But stray wildlife and homeless people and Greek fishermen are telling me I shouldn't fall in love with you, which I could very easily do with little to no provocation. And in the part of my psyche that books all my travel arrangements to hell, I'm trying to figure out if there's a loophole to the not-falling-in-love moratorium that would still let me fuck your brains out and just end up being pen pals.

"Now why do I think *you're* the one who's lying?" she asks pleasantly.

"I don't know. Maybe you're psychic too."

"You think so?"

"I was being facetious, but hey, why not?"

"Maybe I *am* psychic. You know, sometimes I know who's calling on the phone even before I pick it up."

"So do I, Mysterio. It's known as caller ID."

"I mean *without* looking at the caller ID, ass-basket."

"Such language from a delicate young lady. Okay, psychic girl, dazzle me with your powers of mind-reading ability."

She considers what would be a good demonstration. "All right, think of a card from an ordinary deck of cards. Picture it in your mind. Have you got it?"

"Yes," I say.

"I will tell you what your card is, simply by reading your thoughts. Let me concentrate."

Out of the corner of my eye, I see her concentrating. It borders on adorable. She scrunches up her face and closes her eyes tightly. From the intense expression on her features, she is either concentrating or defecating. I sincerely hope it is the former and not the latter.

"Is your card ... the three of spades?"

A look of wonder visits my face. "Yes ... yes, it is."

She looks amazed and delighted. "It is? I got it on the first try?!"

I can't do it to her. "No. Actually, it wasn't really the three of spades."

She smacks my arm, harder—I think—than the infraction deserves. "Then why did you tell me it was?"

"I wanted you to feel like you were doing well. Didn't it feel good when you thought you got it right?"

"Come on, be serious. Tell me the truth. Is it the jack of diamonds?"

"No."

"Six of hearts?"

"No."

"Ace of clubs?"

"Nope."

"Ten of diamonds?"

"Sorry."

"You're not using a tarot deck or something, are you? I won't give up after thirty guesses and you'll tell me your card was the five of tentacles, will you?"

"It's pentacles, and no. Regular card. I know the rules."

"Two of hearts?"

"No."

"King of spades?"

"Nope."

"Well, fine. Maybe I'm not psychic then. What was the card?"

"Pernell Roberts."

"That's *so* not funny. Really, what was it?"

"Five of diamonds."

"Shit."

"But, ironically enough, the diamond looks a little like a pentacle, so your tarot card guess was very close to my card."

She looks terribly disappointed.

"What's so wrong with not being psychic?" I ask her.

"Nothing," she says quietly. "It would just be … interesting. Like you."

"You can't tell me that you think you're uninteresting."

"If I tell you what my biggest fear is, do you promise you won't make fun of me?"

I'm almost offended that she has to even ask such a thing, but I'm simultaneously flattered that she's willing to share this with me, so I answer, "Of course."

It takes her a few moments to find the words. They are spoken with the tone of a confession. "I'm so afraid of dying without ever making a difference."

And there it is. The fear that so many millions have felt throughout human history, but so often feels unique to the person feeling it. A fear I myself have felt many times in my life, times when I was sure that I would never make a difference, never mean anything to anyone. Now, here is someone who shares that fear—probably never realizing that she has the potential to make a great deal of difference.

"I understand, Rebecca. Better than you may realize."

"But look at you. This journey you're on. Every day, you're saving a human life. God, what does that feel like?"

"I don't know if I could put it into words," I tell her honestly. "But you're right. Every time someone listens to the message I deliver, I feel like I've changed a very small part of history."

"I want to feel that in my life," she says.

"You're forgetting one important thing." She looks at me quizzically. "One of those people I saved was you. I don't fully understand this mission I'm on, but I have to believe that means you're meant for something important."

She brightens at the prospect. "You really think so?"

"It makes sense. Otherwise, why send me all over creation to warn people?"

"Well," she says, "there are those who believe that every human life is valuable, no matter what the individual is doing with it."

I shoot her an incredulous look. "Oh, come on."

"Yeah, well, I didn't say *I* believe it."

"Thank you," I say. "Yes, it would be lovely to think that there's value in every human life. But look at the world. Six billion plus. I'm willing to accept that there's *potential* in every human life, but when you choose to throw away that potential, all bets are off. Do you know why you have that worst fear of yours? That fear that so many people everywhere feel every day?" She shakes her head. "It's because dying without making a difference is the default situation."

"Explain?"

"We go through our lives every single day, searching for Meaning with a capital M. What is the meaning of life? We shout this to the heavens, to a God who may or may not be picking up his voicemail messages. And in the meantime, most of us scurry about, to our jobs, to our homes, to our TV sets and our karaoke bars and our Internet porn, and we miss the bigger picture. There's meaning everywhere, and 99.999 percent of the time, we're not even looking at it." And then it hits me. "Holy shit."

"What?" she asks, apparently fascinated at my diatribe.

"I think I know why I was chosen."

"You do? Why?"

"I wasn't psychic or anything like that before this whole thing started. I couldn't tell you that your card was the two of clubs if you were holding it up in front of my face. But then, from out of nowhere, I get these messages, and I realize that I've been picked to deliver them. And I realize now, just this minute as I'm talking to you, that it started right about the same time I truly understood the things I was just telling you about. Don't you see? I wasn't picked because I had some special gift. I was picked because I saw through the bullshit and realized a truth that I would need in order to do the job."

As I voice this thought, it makes infinite sense to me, and it is a colossal relief. For months, I have been repeating the *why me* mantra without any sense of an explanation. But here it is, and what it took was someone to tell it to.

"So what will you do, now that you know?" she asks.

"I don't know. I guess I'll keep doing what I've been doing. Knowing *why* doesn't change what I have to do. It just gives me some much-needed understanding, and for that, I thank you."

"Me?" she says, surprised. "What did I do?"

"You gave me someone to tell it to."

She smiles at this. "Well, you're welcome." After several very peaceful seconds, she then asks, "Can we stop somewhere for dinner soon? I'm getting hungry."

"Reach under your seat," I tell her.

She reaches down and her hand finds plastic. With a loud crinkle, the object emerges, and she looks at the bag in distaste. "Funyuns? Eww. I wouldn't give these to an animal."

"Well, see now, I would, and there's the fundamental difference between us. Although I've learned that deer don't like them."

Given the tightness of time, dinner has to be delivered via drive-thru. I have never been a huge cheeseburger fan, either in or out of paradise, but it's what Rebecca is craving, and since time is tight, we certainly don't have the luxury of choice. So, fun on a bun it is.

"How much longer until we're there?" she asks me between french fries.

"About two hours, at this rate," I tell her. "Why, you getting restless?"

"It's just been awhile since I've taken a long car trip. And you have to admit that this has not been the most normal two days I've had lately."

"Well, considering that I just met you yesterday, I can't say what the baseline level of excitement or normalcy is in your life. You may be like a Bond girl; I don't know. The life of an exotic dancer is probably very exciting."

She pauses a moment before deciding, "That bothers you, doesn't it?"

"What bothers me?"

"My chosen occupation. You get this … *thing* in your voice when either one of us talks about it. Why does it bother you?"

"It doesn't bother me. Why would it? I'm not your father; I'm not your brother; I'm not your …" The word doesn't come easily.

"Boyfriend?" she prompts.

"Right. I'm not that. So, no, it doesn't bother me."

"Then why do you get that thing in your voice?"

"What *thing?*"

"The thing that's there right now. The high thing with the growly thing."

I deliberately ease my tone of voice back down to normal conversation—at least normal for being in a convertible at highway speed. "Rebecca, there is no thing. What you do to earn a living is entirely your business. Now you look disappointed. You *want* it to bother me?"

"A little, yeah."

"I swear, if I live to be a hundred years old …" *or, you know, until tomorrow,* "I will never understand women. Okay, I know I'll regret this, but I'll ask: Why do you want me to be bothered that you were an exotic dancer?"

"Because we're friends, and friends care about what the other person does for a living."

This is getting more unbelievable by the minute. "I cared enough … before I'd even met you, let me add … to drive 1,200 miles and convince you to give up this profession. Doesn't that say something?"

"Ah, but did you do that because you cared about me or because it was your assignment?"

Well, okay, she's got me there. Lying won't work, since she already knows the answer. "Because it was my assignment."

"There, you see?"

"But once I started to talk to you, I did begin to care. And I wanted you to follow what the message said."

She looks surprised. "You mean that?"

"Yes."

"Can I ask you a difficult question?" she says.

"Might as well. It's how this conversation is going."

"When you saw me on stage with my clothes off, did you want to fuck me?"

In the hall of fame of difficult questions, currently dominated by such gems as *"Does this outfit make me look fat?"* and *"When will you pay me back the money you owe me?"* and of course *"Whose lipstick is this on your penis?"* this was the crowning gem of all difficult questions. It was the granddaddy of all traps, to boot. Say yes, and I come across as King Perv, reducing her to an object of sexual desire after thirty seconds of our acquaintance. Say no, and I risk making her feel ugly, unwanted, or worse, unsuccessful at her work. And unlike Final Jeopardy, I don't even have thirty seconds to come up with an answer, because delay reads as weaseling out of it.

"I don't know. Probably, yes." I brace myself for the consequences. "Does that make me an asshole? If it does, you can tell me. I've been called worse."

"It doesn't make you an asshole. It makes you a guy."

That's a relief. I stave off further parlay. "In the name of decency, can I please request that you not ask the follow-up question about whether I still want to fuck you? Because you're a very nice girl and it's been a very long day and I think that anything I say can and will be used against me, so for the sake of what's left of my honor, I'm going to plead the Fifth."

"Objection sustained," she says politely. "You may step down."

"Change that to *fall down,* and I'll take you up on that."

"You want me to drive for a while?" she asks.

"Would you mind taking a shift?"

"Sure I will."

"Thank you. If you can get us just shy of the Atlanta metro area, I'll do the city driving."

"Cool. Pull into that rest area," she says. "I could stand to pee."

"No," I correct her, "if you could *stand* to pee, you'd be a guy."

"Ha ha. Very funny. Don't quit your day job."

The rest area is a welcome relief. I can and do stand to pee, literally and figuratively, after which I dispose of the fast-food debris in the trash bin, before it has a chance to fly out of the open car at highway speed. With a little less than two hours to go before we reach Atlanta, I am grateful for the opportunity to let Rebecca drive for a while. I am also painfully aware of how tight our time schedule is. Barring any traffic snarls, we should arrive at our destination with just a few minutes to spare. The forces that have brought me here know it too, and have graciously pointed out to me which route to take into town. They have also very kindly given me a toothache as a reminder of the urgency of this mission—as if I could think of much else at the moment.

Mercifully, she is quick to return from the ladies' room, and slips behind the wheel swiftly as I take the passenger's seat. She fires up the Sebring's engine, backs out of the parking space, and we are back on the road once more. It is early evening now, and there is still some daylight. I'm not sure if there will be any left by the time we get there; I hope there is, as it will make my job easier, although the streets of a major city are usually well lit at night.

"Do we have a plan?" Rebecca asks me, four miles past our rest stop.

"A plan for what?"

"For how things are going to go down tonight. From what you told me, it sounds dicey at best, flat-out dangerous, more like. I just wanted to know if we have a plan of action or if we're making this up as we go."

"We'll switch drivers just outside the city limits. Then, a few blocks from the spot, we'll switch back, so you can take the car and yourself to safety."

"That's silly," she decides. "Just let me drive us the rest of the way."

"Are you sure? I don't want you to drive in city traffic …"

"It's not a big deal. I've done it before, and we'll get there long after rush hour. It wastes time to switch drivers twice. I'm fine; I'm not tired. This way, you can navigate and I can drop you off once we get there."

"All right, thank you. And when you do, I want you far away from me, from what I have to do out there."

"Unh-uh," she replies. "I need to be able to see you and hear you. If something goes wrong, I want to be able to get you out of there in a hurry."

I shake my head in disapproval. "I don't like it. I don't like putting you in harm's way."

"Don't worry. I'll be far enough away that nothing will happen to me."

"Rebecca … if the worst happens … I have a small brown notebook in my travel bag. In it is my pertinent information. Contacts, phone numbers, my attorney's information—"

"Please don't talk like that. I understand what you're saying, and I'll do what has to be done. But I don't want to think about the worst happening."

"All right, fair enough. We'll think positively."

I hear genuine concern in her voice, and it touches me. I know she is scared, but not for herself. Nothing I say at this point can make it better, since I share that fear. So for many long minutes, we continue up Interstate 75 in silence, each of us very focused on the job ahead.

Through my navigating, she manages the streets of Atlanta with no problem, which is no small feat in a city where you can turn from Peachtree onto Peachtree, and take it to Peachtree, where you take a right onto Peachtree until it dead ends into Peachtree.

Closer and closer we draw to the destination, and time is very short. There will be no time to spare and no wiggle room if we don't find exactly who and what we're looking for.

"Turn right here," I tell her, and she does.

"How much further?" she asks.

"Less than two blocks. Drive slow, drive slow."

"What are we looking for?"

"Silver Lexus, four-door."

"I don't see it, Tristan."

"You just drive. I'll find the car." My eyes scan every vehicle parked on either side of the street. I know the car I'm looking for will be parked. But where?

Rebecca takes us through an intersection, and then I see it. Silver Lexus four-door, just like the image in my mind.

"Son of a bitch," I say. "That's our guy. That's him. He's heading for the car now. Stop the car. Stop the car and let me out."

I get out before she even comes to a complete stop. "Now go!" I warn her. "Be far away from this."

She pulls over to a parking spot, several hundred yards from the Lexus but not nearly far enough away for my comfort. I sprint as best I can toward the Lexus, hoping to intercept its owner in time. The man is tall, well-dressed, distinguished-looking, and yet conveys an air that he is dangerous and not to be toyed with. He has his keys in his hand, and as I draw close enough to talk with him, he is only ten feet from the Lexus.

"Mr. Casner!" I call. "Mr. Jeffrey Casner!"

He stops in his tracks and turns to look at me, surprised by my haste and my unfamiliar face. "That's right," he says. "Who are you?"

I pause a moment to catch my breath. I'm not used to running. "My name is John Diamond. I'm here to give you a message."

"Is that so?" he says. "Who's it from?"

"I don't know. I was just ordered to give a message to Jeffrey Casner at this place and time."

"And just how did you know that I would be at this place at this time? You following me?"

"No."

"You having me watched?"

"No, it's nothing like that. I've never met you, and I have no interest in this apart from giving you this message."

"Okay, what's the message?"

"Don't get in your car."

Disbelief and annoyance visit his face. "What did you just say?"

"Don't get in your car. It isn't safe."

"Oh, really?"

"Yes. It's important that you move away from the car."

"Fuck you," he says. "What's your fuckin' problem? You trying to scare me?"

"No, it's not like that. I'm trying to warn you."

He looks simultaneously amused and angry. He calls out to anyone within earshot, in a mocking tone. "Hey, somebody call a cop. This guy's threatening to kill me!"

"Please keep your voice down."

This just invites him to speak louder. "Keep my voice down? You got some nerve. What are you gonna do, take a swing at me?"

"What? No, of course not."

"Well, let me tell you something, John Diamond or whoever the fuck you are: I ain't scared of you or anybody in your piece-of-shit organization. So you can go right back to Wolfson or whoever sent you, and tell 'em that they can kiss my fuckin' ass if they think they're gonna intimidate me. Go to hell and fuck you too, you little asshole errand boy."

Without another word (thankfully, given the nature of the ones he's already shared) he unlocks the doors to the Lexus, opens the driver's door, and sits down behind the wheel. Instantly, the realization hits me: *He's going to start the car. I've failed.*

In less than a heartbeat, I am turning on my heels. Almost unconsciously, I hear myself shouting, "Rebecca, take cover!" And as I run as fast as I can for the Sebring, I see her duck down as much as possible, while she activates the lever to raise the car's top. At this point, I don't look back, I can't look back; I know exactly what is going to happen, what I couldn't stop from happening.

Casner puts the key in the ignition and turns it. Though I am at least twenty feet from the Lexus at this moment, the shockwave from the explosion propels me forward, face first. I leave my feet and take to the air, putting my hands out in front of me instinctively. Flying, falling, flying, falling, falling, falling ... nothing.

Yes, that's correct—nothing. Unconsciousness comes to greet me like an unwelcome relative. Until this moment, I have never in my life lost consciousness through violent means. And from what I'm feeling, I don't recommend it. It's not like drifting off to a welcome slumber after a long, satisfying day. It's more a swift progression along the lines of: *shit, this hurts; hey, I'm flying; is that pavement?* And then the aforementioned nothing. Now, I know that in detective novels, the hero is always getting knocked unconscious with some damn thing or other. And then a scene dissolve later, he wakes up with "Oh, my head" or something equally heroic.

For me, on that downtown Atlanta street, there is no dissolve, no heroic wake-up line. Just a face full of asphalt and a world of hurt. I honestly don't know how long I was out, but I don't think it could have been very long. When I am able to see and hear again, I am aware of emergency vehicles: a fire truck hosing down Casner and his car. Two police cars are between me and the Lexus, and two more block off the street from traffic.

Ever so slowly, I try to make my way to a standing position. Suddenly I feel something under my arm—a hand of someone assisting me to stand. At first, I think it is Rebecca, but I don't see her. The Sebring is still parked where she left it, with the top up. I can only hope she's inside. I look to my side and realize that it is an Atlanta police officer who has helped me up.

"It's okay," I say to him over the ringing that's filling my ears. "I think I'm all right. I'm not hurt."

Once I stand, he continues to hold on to my arm. I look him in the eyes, curious as to why he's still holding me even after I'm on my feet. The answer I get is a million miles from anything I want or expect to hear. "You're under arrest for the murder of Jeffrey Casner."

Chapter 7

"I'm under *what?*"

He puts my hands behind my back and informs me, "You have the right to remain silent. If you give up the right to remain silent, anything you say can and will be used against you in a court of law. You have the right to an attorney, and to have that attorney present during questioning. If you cannot afford an attorney, one will be appointed for you at no cost to yourself. Do you understand these rights as I have read them to you?"

"Yes," I say, quite annoyed. I know the Miranda rights; it's not the first time I've been arrested. What shocks me is that they actually believe I killed Casner. Clearly, they weren't on scene for what took place just minutes ago, or they would have seen me trying to warn him. Everything is happening so quickly, and it would do me no good to try to explain it to them here and now.

I look over at the Sebring. Still no sign of Rebecca, but she must be lying low in there. At the moment, I'm grateful, lest they think she's an accomplice and arrest us both. I only hope she sees me being led off and remembers what I told her about my attorney's information in my bag. Then I glance across the street and see two officers talking to a man in a parking lot. Did someone see the exchange? Is that why I was arrested?

I am unceremoniously stuffed in the back of a police car, head still swimming from the effects of the explosion, and driven to a nearby station house. Events take on a surreal quality, compounded by the mental exhaustion of the past two days. I am fingerprinted, photographed, moved about, talked to, talked at, and deposited in an interrogation room. I'm not sure how much time has passed, but it feels like a lot. And the one thing missing is the phone call. I know enough to know that I'm entitled to my phone call, but they haven't even entertained discussion of it. I can only hope, as I sit alone in an interrogation room (clearly intended to psych me out) that Rebecca has made the call and that Steven Atkinson, attorney-at-law, has the situation in hand.

If nothing else, the time to myself is allowing me to recuperate, both physically and mentally, from the explosion that killed Jeffrey Casner. I failed my assignment; he didn't listen to me and it cost him his life. And while he wasn't going to win any awards for congeniality or humanitarian efforts, I can't help but feel that I'm at least partly responsible for his death. Not nearly as responsible as the son of a bitch who put a bomb in his car, but nonetheless.

Tell that to the police, Tristan old boy, because right now, they think that son of a bitch is you.

My situation is grim, but it's not the first time. I've had a couple of arrests before, minor things like trespassing and disturbing the peace—both related to the assignments I was on, of course. But Steven Atkinson managed to get charges dropped both times. Whether he can do so this time, with a charge of murder looming, is another story.

I can't believe what a crock of shit this charge is. Murder? Really? Yes, yes, to an impartial observer, I was the last person to have words with the deceased. At the crime scene. Seconds before it happened. And the words were heated and pertained to the deceased's impending demise.

I may actually be fucked on this one, come to think of it.

The door to the interrogation room opens, and a man in his late forties enters. He's wearing Dockers and a long-sleeve dress shirt, with a tie ugly enough to suggest that someone bought it for him and he wears it out of politeness, rather than actual fondness for it. He is dressed, it seems, just formally enough to conform to department regulations, and his posture tells of a man who would much rather be in a pair of jeans and an old, well-worn sweatshirt. I feel weariness on him, the mark of a man who had great enthusiasm for his chosen career when he entered it some twenty or more years ago, but has since been brought back to earth by day after day of mundane reality and bureaucratic oppression.

All this before he even opens his mouth to say a word to me. Once the words come, I feel my assessment is right. "You're a complicated man, Mr. Shays," he says.

"So I've been told," I respond, trying to sound cooperative and not wiseass.

"I'm Lieutenant Fogle. I'm the detective in charge of this case, such as it is."

So are you good cop or bad cop? I wonder silently.

"Can I get you a cup of coffee or some water?" he asks me.

Ah, good cop. I can live with that.

"I'm fine on that front," I tell him, "but I'd really appreciate a chance to call my attorney. I think once we all sit down together, we'll realize that there's been a misunderstanding."

"Your legal advisor is already here," he answers.

This is news to me. *How could Steven already be here, coming from as far away as he did? It's possible that he was on the road and just happened to be near Atlanta when Rebecca called him, but …*

"She's talking with the desk sergeant now," Fogle continues. "She'll be in here momentarily."

"Wait … *She?* But …"

Before I can inquire further about his pronoun choice, the door to the room opens, and in walks my legal advisor. I try not to do an actual cartoon-worthy double take when I see Rebecca enter, dressed in the most formal outfit she has brought with her—which amounts to slacks and a white blouse—and carrying a briefcase … *my* briefcase from the trunk of the Sebring. Without thinking, I stand up quickly.

"Sit down," Fogle and Rebecca say simultaneously. So I sit.

With an air of confidence I have yet to encounter from her, she strides in and owns the room. Hand outstretched, she introduces herself to my interrogator. "Rebecca Traeger, legal advisor to Mr. Shays."

"Detective Lieutenant Eric Fogle. Good to meet you, Ms. Traeger."

She sits next to me. I'm sure I look astonished.

"I'm a bit surprised you were able to be here so quickly," Fogle says to her, "seeing as how Mr. Shays isn't from Atlanta."

"Fortunately, I was in the area. It's a good thing, too," she adds, looking at a single typewritten page she brought in with her. "I'd like to get Mr. Shays released this evening, as I happen to know that he has some important matters to see to."

Fogle seems put off by her boldness. "I'm afraid it's not that simple, Ms. Traeger. There's a charge of first-degree murder …"

"Simple?" she says with an icy look at him. "I think we're swimming in a sea of oversimplification here, Detective. I've read through this arrest report, and I'm shaking my head at why my client is even here. Last time I checked, habeas corpus does still apply in Georgia, does it not?"

It's a fascinating performance, I have to admit. If I weren't the star of the grisly state-sponsored execution to follow, I would be on my feet and applauding.

Fogle's patience, meanwhile, is starting to wear thin. "Now, see here, Ms. Traeger. There's compelling evidence. I have an eyewitness at the scene who saw Mr. Shays talking heatedly with Jeffrey Casner just before the explosion. This eyewitness saw your client running away from the vehicle seconds before it blew up. Now, we're still putting together all the pieces, but with all due respect to your habeas corpus, in my jurisdiction, that's called prima facie evidence, and it's enough to hold Mr. Shays—without bail—until a preliminary hearing can be held."

He's good; I'll give him that.

She switches tactics. "Detective, I apologize. I meant no disrespect to you or your department. It's been a long day, and the news of Mr. Shays's arrest came as a surprise to me. I want what you want: the capture and prosecution of Jeffrey Casner's killers. I just need to spend a little time with you this evening to help you see that there's no way Mr. Shays could have committed this crime. If you're willing to work with me tonight, I'm hoping we can rule him out as a suspect and clear the slate to find who did this."

He thinks about it for a moment. "All right. I'm willing to listen."

"Do you have the witness statement?" she asks.

"I imagine it'll be done by now. I'll have to go get it. Wait here, please."

He gets up and leaves Rebecca alone with me in the room. She smiles broadly at me. "Hi," she says pleasantly.

"Hi? You're giving me *hi?* What are you doing here?"

"Representing you, obviously."

I suddenly remember where we are, a room known for a lack of privacy. "Wait a second. We shouldn't be talking in here. Someone could be watching."

"I checked the room that looks in on this one. No one's in there. Fogle is the only one here who's working on the case at the moment."

"I see. And you're representing me?"

"Yep."

"Are you out of your mind? I've been arrested for murder!"

She holds up the arrest report in front of me. "Duh."

"I asked you to call my attorney …"

"I *did* call your attorney. He's in the Bahamas right now, and will be for the next week. I kinda figured you didn't want a public defender, so I hid in the car until the cops left, then drove over here after a reasonable amount of time had passed, and here I am."

"Here you are." I lower my voice to an emphatic whisper. "Might I remind you that you're not an attorney!"

"Relax," she says, "relax. Before I left school, I was pre-law. I've taken a bunch of criminal justice and criminal procedure classes. I know what I'm doing. Besides, this case is so open-and-shut, you don't need your expensive attorney. I can get you out of here. And just so you know, I didn't tell them I was your attorney; I told them I'm your legal advisor, which I am. I couldn't represent you in court, but I'm allowed to counsel you in this situation. So chill. I've got it covered."

I'm stunned by how calm she is and how reasonable her explanation sounds. If it's an act, it's a hell of a good one. "You really know what you're doing?" I ask her.

"Completely."

I pause in acceptance of her aid. "I'm glad you're okay," I say quietly.

"I'm glad you're okay too. That explosion was scary. And kinda cool. But mostly scary."

"I fucked up," I say to her. "I couldn't save him."

"You tried. That's what matters. You tried to save him, but he wouldn't listen."

At this inopportune moment, Detective Fogle returns with the typed witness statement and hands it to Rebecca. She thanks him and begins reading. Though she tries hard to keep a poker face, I know her body language well enough to know by now that this document is good news for us. She finishes reading and looks over at Fogle, who is still standing opposite us on his side of the table.

"This is it?" she asks. "This is all?"

"You can see that the witness was on the same block, and swore that he saw Mr. Shays having a heated argument with Jeffrey Casner, then running away from the vehicle right before it exploded."

"What I'm missing here, Detective, is the substance of that argument. Nowhere in this report does the witness state what was said by either Mr. Shays or Mr. Casner."

Fogle looks less than pleased at this. "Yeah, I asked about that. He was too far away to hear what was said."

"And you're accepting this as a valid witness statement?"

"Absent any other eyewitnesses with information to the contrary, he's what we have. He saw the exchange. He saw Mr. Shays running from the scene before the car blew up."

"Which would be consistent with Mr. Shays's statement," Rebecca says, "that he was warning Jeffrey Casner *not* to get into his car. He knew that someone had planted an explosive device, and he was acting as a Samaritan to try to save Casner's life."

"Then how did he know about the bomb?" Fogle asks her. "Knowledge suggests complicity. An accessory before the fact."

"His knowledge of the circumstances is not key to the chain of evidence," she argues. "Where's the means? Where's the motive? My client will swear under oath that he had no prior relationship with Jeffrey Casner before tonight, eliminating any suggestion of motive."

"You know, I'm right here," I remind them both. "You might consider asking me some of these questions."

Fogle nods a little. "All right, Mr. Shays. As you said, you're right here. Let's assume for a moment that you didn't plant that bomb."

"Great," I say, "can I go?"

That elicits a little laugh from him. "Humor me. Stick around. If you didn't plant it and you aren't working with the people who did, how did you know it was there?"

I look at him, then at Rebecca. She less-than-discreetly makes a head gesture that screams *tell him,* and I have to agree that I don't have much choice.

"For the past two years, I have been gifted with foreknowledge of some events," I tell him. "And with that foreknowledge comes an obligation to prevent certain tragedies from happening. One of those tragedies was the murder of Jeffrey Casner. I learned about it early this afternoon, and I hurried here to try to stop it from happening. I got here just in time to talk to him, but he wouldn't listen to my warning, and he got in the car anyway. The heated argument we had was him telling me he didn't want to listen to my warning. I was running away from there because I knew I'd failed, and I was trying to get to safety."

There is a long pause as he takes this in, which doesn't bode well for me. The look on his face is pure disbelief, and after a few seconds, his words confirm it. "That's it?" he says. "That's the best you've got?"

Rebecca tries to stop him. "Detective …"

"Let him talk," I say quietly. "It's all right."

Fogle continues. "I was ready to listen to a lot of possibilities. Alibis, explanations, maybe a suggestion of who did this. But that?" He exhales while shaking his head. "So you're what? You're psychic now, is that it?"

"In a sense, yes," I answer. "I'm not a fortune teller or anything like that. I just have to do this, and I don't know why."

He sighs and runs his fingers through his hair. "I don't know what to do with you, Mr. Shays. You seem like a good guy. I'd really like to believe that you're some kind of … I dunno, guardian angel, maybe. I want to believe that you were there on that street to save Casner's life. But then I look at the evidence. I have you at the scene, seconds before the explosion, arguing with Casner. I have you running away from the scene. I have the fact that Casner wasn't even supposed to be in Atlanta tonight, but he canceled his trip to Florida at the last minute, and nobody knows why."

"He did?" I ask.

"That's right. He was supposed to be in the Keys, fishing, but for some reason, he stayed in Atlanta."

Rebecca and I exchange a meaningful glance. *The Days Inn—the room cancellation by the man from Atlanta. Could it be him?*

Fogle continues. "I've got you with no alibi. No one to put you anywhere else at the time the bomb was placed."

I see it in Rebecca's eyes that she wants to be that alibi, but she can't risk saying that she was with me beforehand. Then, something else appears in her expression, an idea, maybe.

"Wait a second," she interrupts. "You said *at the time the bomb was placed*. How do you know what time the bomb was placed?"

"It was triggered by the car's ignition," Fogle explains. "And we know he was at the health club three hours earlier, so he couldn't have been parked on that street for more than three hours. The bomb had to be placed after he parked it there. So we have a range of time."

"That's it," she says. "That's it. Tristan, give me your credit card."

"Why?" I ask.

"Just trust me."

I pull out my wallet. "Which card?"

"Whichever one you've used today."

I pull out the gold MasterCard I used to buy meals and pay for hotels, and hand it to her. She takes it and hands it directly to Fogle. "Detective, please call the bank's customer service number. Tell them who you are, and ask them for a detailed transaction record for the past twenty-four hours. You'll see that the card was used in person to buy meals in central Florida during the timeframe when the bomb was placed. Please, Detective. This is the evidence my client needs to establish an alibi."

Fogle looks at her and at the card. "Give me a few minutes," he says, and then he leaves the room.

Once he is gone, Rebecca turns to face me, positively aglow. "Ta da!" she beams.

"Ta da?" I repeat.

"This is it. This is your alibi. You were nowhere near Atlanta during those hours, and the credit card records will prove it. He'll have to let you go."

"Credit cards can be used by phone or online," I remind her. "This might not be the alibi you're hoping for."

"The bank keeps a record of whether the card was used in person or electronically. Once they find out you were nowhere near Atlanta at the time, you'll be set."

Now I'm officially impressed. "You really know what you're doing."

"Kinda cool, isn't it? You saved me, I saved you. Now we're even."

"With all due respect to your optimism, I'll wait until Fogle comes back and tells me I'm free to go."

Three minutes later, the door opens and Fogle walks in with my credit card in hand. "You're free to go," he says to me.

I can't believe it. "What?"

"Ms. Traeger was right. Your credit card usage means you weren't in Atlanta when this happened, so you can't be held for murder. Your status has been changed to 'person of interest in this case.'"

Flattering as that sounds ... "What does that mean?" I ask. "What happens next?"

"It means you don't have to remain in custody tonight," he says. "You'll need to stay in Atlanta overnight, while we look into a few more things. I'll also want a phone number where you can be reached tonight if we have questions." I write my cell number down and hand it to him. I have to pause a moment to remember the number; I almost never use the thing.

"In the morning," he continues, "I want you to give me a call at this number." He hands me his business card. "At that point, I'll tell you if you're clear to be on your way."

"Thank you, Detective," I say to him.

"There's still some things I want to know," he tells me. "Top of the list is how you knew this was going to happen, and how you knew to be there just in time."

"It's nothing I can explain," I tell him honestly. "Sometimes I just know what's going to happen to people, and I try to keep it from happening."

"Tell me this," he says, "am I going to live to see retirement?"

I reach out and take hold of his left forearm with my hand, looking deeply and intently into his eyes. Five seconds pass, then ten. A sober look crosses my face. "No," I say quietly. "I'm sorry, but you won't."

With that, Rebecca and I leave the interrogation room and make our way toward the exit, through the squad room. "That was freaky," she says to me. "You mean to say you actually know that Fogle is going to die before retirement?"

"No," I answer calmly, "I can't see that kind of thing."

She looks confused. "Then why did you—?"

"I just don't like the guy."

She tries hard to contain her astonished laughter. "You are *so evil!*" she says.

"Thank you. I was hoping you might not say that quite so loud as we're leaving the police station where I've just been released as a murder suspect."

"Oh, sorry. Good point."

Chapter 8

It feels good to be back in the fresh air outside of the police station. Though I know I am innocent and the department's case is weak, I also know that innocent men have gone to prison ... or worse ... for crimes they didn't commit. Rebecca has saved my bacon.

"Long night, huh?" she says.

"Long *day*," I reply.

"Well, we have to stay in Atlanta. You want to find a little place to spend the night?"

"No," I say. "I want to find a big place to spend the night."

Tonight is all about a good night's sleep, after everything that's happened today. Rebecca leads us to the parking garage where she stashed the Sebring; we pay the car's ransom and drive about a mile to the Atlanta Hilton downtown. I don't even care what it costs. Tonight I need comfort, elegance, and cleanliness.

I park under the overhang outside of the office, and we both walk up to the reception desk. A very proper, very pleasant-looking woman greets us. "Welcome to the Hilton. Checking in?"

"Yes," I say.

"Do you have a reservation?" she asks.

"No," I reply, "but we're hoping you have two rooms ..."

Rebecca quickly interrupts. "One room. We just need one room, with two queen beds, if you have it." I look at her with curiosity and surprise, and she says to me, "I want to be there, in case something happens. A call or a new assignment."

"Are you sure?" I ask her.

"Yes, I'm sure."

The desk clerk checks the computer and finds what we're looking for. "Just one night?"

"To start with, yes," I reply.

"It's 279 for the night," she says. She could have said ten thousand and I would have agreed to it.

I bring out my gold MasterCard, the card that kept me from having considerably grimmer accommodations tonight, and hand it to her. She runs the card and presents me with the form to fill out.

"I hope you enjoy your stay with us tonight," she says sincerely.

"I think it's a pretty safe bet," I answer.

Ten minutes later, the Sebring is in a proper parking spot, and Rebecca and I are in our sixteenth-floor room, with a view of downtown Atlanta greeting us through the window. The room is immaculate and even smells good. A mini-bar refrigerator holds the promise of indulgent, overpriced goods, and I want every single one of them.

Rebecca gravitates to the window. "Look at this view!" she gushes.

"I'm just happy for a window with no bars on it," I tell her. "And I have you to thank for that. You were pretty incredible back there."

She bobs her head, grinning a bit. "Yeah, I kinda was, wasn't I?"

"So will you continue on with law when you go back to school?"

She is caught off guard by the question. "I really hadn't thought about it. I suppose I will. With everything that's gone on the past two days, I kind of put school out of my mind. Still, it felt good to use what I learned."

"Definitely an A-plus on your practical exam tonight." With that, I go to my briefcase and open it. I reach inside and discreetly get what I need. Once it's finished, I tear it out and hold the piece of paper out to her. "I want you to have this," I tell her.

Quite surprised, she looks at the check. "Five thousand dollars? Are you kidding me?"

"Not in the least. I figure that's fair recompense for keeping me out of prison. I assure you, my attorney would get at least that much, and would've taken longer to spring me. Consider it your first legal fee. Use it to pay for school."

She's visibly stunned by my gift. "Tristan ... I can't ... I can't take your money."

"But you've earned it," I insist.

"What I did tonight—helping you that way—I think that was the greatest feeling I've ever had in my life. And as far as money for school goes, my father said if I needed money, he'd pay for the whole thing anytime I wanted to go back. So ... thank you for this. Really, I mean that." She tears up the check and hands it back to me. "But you have to believe me that the end result was reward enough."

Just when I think I'm starting to figure her out ...

"Fair enough," I tell her, "but if you change your mind, I can write you another one."

"Thank you," she says.

"Well, now that the legal part of our evening is over, would you mind terribly if I took the first shower?" I ask.

"Be my guest."

There are baths and showers in mythology and legend that are said to have magical, otherworldly, even healing powers. All of them pale in comparison to the feeling of hot water and tiny hotel soap upon my body this night. Bear in mind that my day began in Marathon, Florida, included a trip to Tarpon Springs, far too many hours spent driving, then arrival in Atlanta, watching a man get blown up while nearly being blown up myself, followed by two hours in a warm police station. This shower is epic. Songs could be written about this shower. When at last I emerge, I feel almost human again.

After I receive a playful and much-deserved teasing by my traveling companion about being in there for so long, she takes her turn in the mystic waters. Though she doesn't spend as much time in there as I did, she does take a leisurely shower, giving me time to change into a T-shirt and boxer shorts and then look out at the lights of the city. A few minutes later, she joins me at the window, dressed as she was the night before, and looking just as good now.

"Feel better?" I ask.

"Yeah. How about you?"

"Amazingly enough, I do."

"Please tell me every day isn't like this for you," she says.

"No, this one was pretty extreme, even for me. But hey, look at where we are: It's just after midnight, we're safe, we've got a great room with an amazing view. And my legal counsel helped me to beat the rap, so that's something."

"Well, it kind of helped that you weren't guilty."

"Would you have defended me if I was?"

"Hmm, an ethical question. I don't know, did you have a good reason for doing it?"

"He needed killin'."

"Ah, the Texas murder defense. Interesting. Yes, I suppose I'd still defend you. You're an upstanding citizen, and he was clearly shady."

"Yeah," I say quietly, "I get that feeling too."

"Who do you think killed him?" she asks, suddenly serious.

"I don't know. He mentioned somebody named Wolfson, and some unspecified 'organization.' I think this guy was a criminal—maybe organized crime—and some rival group had him eliminated."

"You remember what Fogle said about Casner's trip being canceled? His fishing trip to the Keys? We got that room in Marathon last night because a man canceled—a man from Atlanta, the desk clerk said."

"That could be anybody," I remind her.

"But what if it *was* him?" she asks. "What if they're watching us? Following us? This could be the danger that you were sent to warn me about."

"What would they want with you? You've never met these people."

"I know that, but the way things are happening ... maybe I've done something to them and I don't even know it. It scares me, not knowing."

"I understand. But even on the off chance it is related to you, we're staying ahead of them."

She steps away from the window and over toward one of the beds, standing at the foot of it. "If Casner *was* the threat," I say, "then I doubt that I would also be sent to try to protect him. This may all be coincidence."

"I don't even know what to think anymore."

I walk over to her and put my arms around her in a comforting way. She accepts and puts her arms around me, holding on tightly to me. I'm a few inches taller, so her head ends up on my shoulder. Her hair smells wonderful, like fruit and flowers, thanks to the fancy shampoo the hotel provides. In the silence of the room, I can hear her breathing. I don't want to let go, and I absolutely don't have the words to tell her that I'm almost as scared as she is. What I've seen today will be with me for the rest of my life. Right now, she needs reassurance.

"I'll do everything I can to keep you safe," I whisper to her.

In response, she lifts her head from my shoulder and looks into my eyes in the half-light of the room. I'm sure there are a thousand things her expression is saying to me, but I can't make them out. All I see is this woman, a stranger to me two days ago, who has now run an emotional marathon with me. She's such a surprise—smart, strong, capable, yet still vulnerable in the way we all are. I wish to God I knew the right thing to say at this moment, to ease us out of this prolonged silence that's been created between us. But as I am searching for those perfect words, Rebecca completely amazes me by moving closer to me and touching her lips to mine.

Every honorable fiber of my being wants me to pull away, but I can't. I'm no virgin, nor am I a naïve prude, but when she kisses me, it feels like nothing I've ever experienced before. It feels right, and I know it's something I've wanted from the first moment I saw her. I return the kiss and initiate many more, on her lips, her face, her neck. I run my eager fingers through the softness of her hair and concentrate on the sensation of how every curve of her body feels pressed against mine as we stand at the foot of that bed. And she kisses me just as enthusiastically, clutching my back and my arms. It is a prolonged moment of insurmountable bliss that suddenly becomes very real when I feel her remove my shirt.

In an instant, I am snapped out of the moment. I step back from her as my T-shirt hits the floor. "What are—" I start. "What are we doing?"

She looks confused. "What do you mean? I thought this is what you wanted. It's what I wanted."

I genuinely don't know what to feel. "I do ... but ... I barely know you."

"Tristan, we've been through more together in the last two days than a lot of couples go through in a year."

Couple? Is that how she sees us?

"I like you," she continues, "and I thought you liked me."

"I do. I really do. This is just … so sudden."

"Is it because of my job?" she asks. "You know I never do this with customers, don't you?"

"No, no, it's nothing like that. I just …" There is an answer within me, and no amount of dancing around it will stop it from being said now. "I just don't know if it's a good idea for me to fall in love with you."

I brace myself for her reaction, fearing how she will respond to that announcement. She steps back and looks at my face. I see a bit of a smile on her lips as she says, "Is that what this hesitation is about? You don't know if you want to fall in love with me?"

"Yes," I answer quietly.

"Tristan," she says gently, "it's not a requirement."

With those four words, it's as if a barrier is lifted. I have no defenses left, nor do I want any. I pull her to me once again and open my lips gently for yet another powerful kiss. When it ends, I look deep into her eyes. "You're beautiful," I say.

"Will you touch me?" she requests. "I've been patient and well-behaved, but now I really want to feel your touch."

I reach down and caress her pretty breasts through her shirt. Her eyes close, and after a few seconds, her nipples rise to meet my fingers. "I love the way you feel," I tell her. I can feel myself getting firm within my shorts. She can feel it too, and she presses her body tighter to mine to savor the sensation. I want her, and I think she feels the same way. But I have to hear it. "Rebecca, do you want me?"

"Yes."

"I just don't want to …" I search for the words. "Get it wrong."

"Then look at me, think of how you feel about me, and do what you've been wanting to do. If it's not something I want … and I can't think of too many things I wouldn't want to do with you right now … I'll tell you."

With that, we both take our sleepwear off and toss it to the floor. Gently out of breath with excitement, we stand facing each other, each looking at the other. She runs her hands up and down my chest, down to my thighs.

She moves her hands together, encircling the rigidity she finds there. I positively shudder with the excitement of her touch.

Rebecca puts her arms around me again, and I put mine around her. Our bodies press together, and I concentrate on how her nipples feel against my chest. She feels very firm and muscular, but still feminine. The dancing she did must be quite a workout. For a moment, I worry how I must feel by comparison, but she quickly puts my fears to rest. "Mmm, you feel so good. I can't wait until our bodies come together."

"What kind of foreplay do you like?" I ask her.

She kisses me again. "Don't overthink it. Just take the time to explore my body. The pleasure I feel comes from just being intimate with you."

For many wonderfully intense moments, I simply hold her, grateful for this opportunity. I watch as she crawls onto the bed and stretches out on her back. I sit at the foot of the bed and raise her legs up, proceeding to kiss the backs of her calves and thighs. I then pay close attention to her beautiful little feet, kissing and sucking, and rubbing them gently against my face. She bends her legs, and I look with great interest at the soft, delicate area between them. She looks so warm, so inviting.

Rebecca notices me looking at her and brings her hand down to touch herself there, silently inviting me to assist her. She's very assertive, so sure of herself.

I slide next to her and lie on my side, bringing my face down to her full, lovely breasts. The nipples are small and very fair. I take each one between my lips and massage it with my mouth. She smiles broadly as I discover the size and taste of her. Before long, little sounds of pleasure escape her lips. "That's so good," she whispers. "Use your teeth. You won't hurt me."

Applying more pressure with my lips and tongue, I bring my teeth together against her nipple, pulling gently against it until it rises sharply inside my mouth. I then turn my attention to her other breast, giving it the same attention.

"Touch me," she says. "Touch me everywhere."

The invitation is most welcome, and I move my hands to her

beautiful body, finding every spot imaginable. I discover the loveliness of her elbows and her wrists, the nape of her neck, the backs of her knees. She responds passionately to touches on her calves and her shoulders. As I caress her, she reaches out to me as well, steadying herself by holding on to my arm or my leg each time we change position on the bed.

Finally, I can hold off no longer, and I reach down between her legs, inserting two fingers deep inside of her. I am greeted by a magnificent warmth, coupled with copious moisture that tells me that she welcomes everything I'm doing. She's so remarkably strong, and as I move my fingers in and out, and from side to side, she grasps them and holds them tightly within her.

I move my fingers faster and faster. Her eyes are closed with the intensity of what she's feeling; her breath is a rapid-fire succession of quick puffs through clenched teeth. "Don't stop," she says. "Don't stop, I'm so close, I'm so close."

I can't think of a single thing that would stop me from what I'm doing. Instead, I continue to touch her, now using both hands to find the places that drive her wild. Thirty seconds pass, then a minute. Then it hits her, and she cries out with pleasure. It is the sound of my lover's passion, and to me it is like the sweetest words sung within the most beautiful music. I can't take my eyes off of her face and the expression that has washed over her.

When at last she relaxes, I take her in my arms and hold her close to me. "I've got you," I whisper. "You're safe."

She emits a breath that almost sounds like a gentle laugh—not of derision but of realization. "Yes … I am."

I hold her for several minutes as she regains her strength. She then sits up and looks me in the eyes. "I want you inside me now."

"Will you be on top?" I ask her. "I want to be able to look at your pretty face."

I lie on the bed, facing up and fully aroused as I watch her approach me. Her eyes display a combination of playfulness and passion. I'm fascinated by her, surprised at the many sides of her, and most of all, turned on at the notion of being with her this way.

She kneels, straddling me. Slowly she lowers her hips, and I slide gently between her thighs. She moans with pleasure. As she leans forward a bit, I reach up and caress her breasts, enjoying their size and shape. My body tingles as she begins moving her hips slowly, rhythmically, up and down.

The feeling is exquisite as we continue to move together this way. I feel my orgasm building and building, until finally it lets go. She moans at the feeling and steadies herself with her hands on my chest as my strength leaves me.

"Was that good?" she asks, sounding genuinely interested in my answer.

"Perfect," I answer.

"Hold me. I want you to hold me."

I get under the covers with her. She presses her soft, naked body up against me, and I wrap my arms tightly around her, trying hard to convey the depth of my happiness at this moment, as much-needed sleep arrives to enfold us.

In the night, I become aware of knocking, even before consciousness returns to me. As I open my eyes, I see that the room is still dark; it's not yet morning. The knocking continues, more persistently. I glance over and see that Rebecca is asleep under the covers. The knocking is at the hotel room door. I get out of bed and put my boxer shorts on, moving to the door. "Who is it?" I ask, hoping not to wake Rebecca.

A voice from behind the door answers, "Detective Fogle, Atlanta Police. Open the door, Mr. Shays."

"Detective Fogle? Is something wrong?"

"Just open the door, please."

I reach for the knob, but it's dark in the room, and I'm still groggy and not very coordinated, and I clearly don't open it fast enough for him. The next thing I know, he's using a key card to open the door himself. As the light from the hallway spills in, I see Fogle enter with two uniformed officers. One of them rushes over to me and grabs me by the arm, holding me roughly. "Suspect is in custody," he says into a radio clipped to his vest.

"Suspect?" I say. "Custody? I don't understand. You have the credit card receipts. You let me go ..."

Apparently ignoring my confused rambling, Fogle says very

officially, "Tristan Shays, you're under arrest for sexual assault against Rebecca Traeger."

The news hits me like a speeding car. *Sexual assault? Who would have told the police that? How would they even know where I was, or that Rebecca and I were together, for that matter?* In utter bewilderment, I turn toward the bed and see that Rebecca is standing at the foot of it, dressed in her sleepwear.

"Detective, thank you so much for coming," she says. "I'm sorry to bother you with this, but I couldn't let him get away with what he did to me."

I feel like everything I understand is collapsing around me. "Get away with what I did? Rebecca ..."

"It's no problem, Miss Traeger," Fogle says. "In the majority of sexual assaults, the victim knows her attacker. It seems Mr. Shays might just get that jail cell after all."

I break free of the officer's hold just enough to face Rebecca. I have to look into her eyes, to find some reason for this, some explanation. All I can manage is a single word: "Why?"

"Why?" she repeats, her tone laced with bitterness and contempt. "You're asking me why, *messenger?*" The word hits me like a physical slap. "You pathetic son of a bitch. You take me from my home, from my job, from everything I know. You drag me with you on your fool's errand, and then you fuck me for your own entertainment, and you ask me why I want to rid myself of you? God, to think I came this close to respecting you. Now I can't stand the sight of you."

Her words wound me more than I thought anything ever could. I realize that she is lost to me, so I turn back to Fogle, trying to plead my case to him. "Detective, please, this is a misunderstanding. Yes, Rebecca and I were intimate last night ..."

"You do remember the part about anything you say being used against you, right?"

"Let me finish. We were intimate, but it was consensual. We talked, and ... and we both felt an attraction to each other. She kissed me, and we shared something very personal, very caring."

Fogle looks over at Rebecca, and she returns the look with a dismissive toss of her head, which silently negates everything I've just said.

"You have to believe me," I tell him.

"I might," he replies, "but we just happen to have another witness who came to us to report sexually inappropriate behavior from you."

This gets worse and worse. "What? Who? I haven't …"

"Bring him in, boys," Fogle says to his team.

Him? The pronoun does not bring me any comfort. I've never in my life been sexually inappropriate with anyone, least of all a *him.*

Before I can ponder it any further, the two uniformed officers return to the hotel room with a familiar face. It is the key deer, the same one who warned me not to fall in love with Rebecca two nights ago. He walks into the room and looks squarely at me.

"That's him," the deer says. "I'd know him anywhere. Look at those eyes. I know a predator when I see one."

"This is a mistake," I say.

"What did he do to you?" Fogle asks the deer, to my growing astonishment.

"He stopped on the road to talk to me. Then he tried to lure me into his car with the promise of Funyuns."

Fogle looks at me and shakes his head. "You sick fuck. I've heard enough. Let's take him in."

It is significant to note at this moment that as I look over at the two uniformed officers, they have transformed into my paternal grandmother and … curiously enough … Pernell Roberts, the latter of whom shakes his head at me disapprovingly and says, "You're not really interested in my career."

I awaken with a start and see that the first rays of morning sunlight are beginning to stream through the window. Rebecca, still by my side, flutters her eyes and yawns. "Are you all right?" she asks sleepily.

"Yeah," I answer quietly. "I just had a bad dream, that's all. I'm fine. Go back to sleep. It's still early."

"It's okay," she says, stretching. "I feel good. I feel rested." She leans in close to me and kisses me. For a moment, I am hesitant and back away slightly. But it's enough that she notices it. "Do you want to talk about the dream?"

Realizing how foolish I must seem, I shake it off. "No, I'm all right," I tell her. "Here, come closer."

She does, and I kiss her again, this time discarding the unpleasantness of the nightmare and welcoming her soft, warm lips to mine. "Thank you for last night," I say.

"Thank *you*," she replies.

"My God, Rebecca … what we shared last night was amazing."

"I know," she says. "I feel like I could stay in this room with you just like this for a month and never get tired of it."

She rises from bed to look out the window as sunrise begins to illuminate the city. "So … today should be the day, then. We can probably make it all the way to Ohio today."

"Is that disappointment I hear in your voice?" I ask.

"Well, you have to admit that after last night, things have changed. Now I'm not so anxious to go."

"Rebecca, I don't know what to say. I didn't expect this to happen. I have to drop you off in Ohio, but it doesn't have to be goodbye."

I start to walk over to her at the window, but my walk is interrupted by a wave of unbelievable pain that seizes my chest with enough strength to throw me to the floor. To a bystander, I imagine it would look quite comical, but I certainly am not laughing. Neither, I notice, is Rebecca, who hurries over to my side and does everything in her power to keep me safe and comfortable.

Through the pain and the incoming message, I am dimly aware of her quietly repeating, "I've got you. You're all right." By now, she recognizes what is happening.

One by one, the details filter in. Names, places, history, directions, and the all-important detail of the mission—what I must do and for whom. The pain and the message continue for a full two minutes, which feels like forever to me. I silently wonder if there will ever come a time when I have accepted enough assignments that they can be sent to me without the accompanying pain and suffering.

At last it subsides, and I am able to raise my head a little. "Are you all right?" Rebecca asks.

"Yes. It still hurts, but I'll be fine."

"Another assignment?"

"Another assignment. And again with some urgency. We have about twelve hours of driving, and only about fifteen hours before everything happens."

"So where are we going?" she asks.

"Wyandotte, Pennsylvania," I reply.

A curious look comes to her face. "Why does that sound so familiar?"

"I suppose it's not terribly far from where your family lives in Ohio. Wyandotte is practically a ghost town. A natural disaster drove off almost everyone eighteen years ago. Now, only one family still lives there, and they're the ones we have to help."

"Why? What's going to happen?"

"In fifteen hours, their house is going to collapse."

Chapter 9

"Fifteen hours?" Rebecca repeats. "That's not much time. I think we should fly there instead of driving."

"I've told you, flying is too risky …"

"Even if the flight is delayed by twelve hours, we'll still get there in plenty of time. I just don't want to see us get there too late."

I begin to pack up the few things I've brought into the room with me, and she does likewise. Maybe this time it's best if I put aside my prejudice and just trust the airlines to get us there. "You're right," I tell her. "Fogle wants me to call him before I leave town. Go ahead and get ready to go. I'll take care of this."

She goes to the bathroom, and I dial the cell phone number that's on the business card the detective gave me last night. I feel bad for calling at this hour, but business is business. After four rings, a tired-sounding Fogle picks up the phone. "Hello?"

"Detective, it's Tristan Shays. I'm sorry for calling you so early, but you asked me to call you before I got on my way, and I need to be going."

He tries to compose himself and speak coherently and professionally. "Is there a particular reason you're wanting to leave so early?"

"Business meeting out of state," I answer. "With your kind approval, of course."

He hesitates a moment. "You're still a person of interest in this matter. The investigation is ongoing, and it would be better for all parties if you stayed in Atlanta for another couple of days."

No, no, you can't be serious. "That's … going to create something of a hardship, Detective. I can come back here if I'm needed, but I'm really counting on your indulgence to give me leave to travel."

"Shays, it's 6:00 in the morning. I'm still in bed here. What you're asking for … it'll take department approval, and that takes time. I need you to sit tight until I clear this with Division."

"Isn't there any way you can expedite this? Please, it's very important."

Irritation begins to creep into his voice. "And I'm telling you this isn't something we can do right here and now. End of discussion. Are we gonna have a problem here?"

Trying not to betray too much emotion in my voice, I reply, "No, Detective, no problem. I understand. Please give me a call on my cell phone when you have the authorization. It's urgent, vitally urgent. Thank you, Detective."

At this moment, I truly wish there was a way to slam down the receiver on a cellular phone. I have to settle for a fierce punching of the END button, after which I shout out "Shit!" loudly enough that it draws Rebecca out of the bathroom.

"What?" she asks, concerned. "What did he say?"

"He wants me to stay in town."

"What? Why?"

"I'm a 'person of interest.' That means they need access to me."

"For how long?" she says.

"Maybe a couple of hours. Maybe a couple of days. In the meantime, the clock is ticking in Pennsylvania."

She approaches me. "What are we going to do?"

"We're gonna go," I answer. "Tell me something as my legal advisor: On a scale of slap-on-the-wrist to balls-in-a-vise, how bad is leaving town when I've been asked not to?"

Rebecca thinks about it for a moment. "Closer to wrist than balls. You're not currently under arrest, but you are still subject to police jurisdiction. Their contact with us is by cell phone, which goes wherever we go. For all they know, we're still in Atlanta. If they call and ask you to come in, we can bullshit and stall for time while we head back here. This could work."

"By going with me," I remind her, "you're assisting a fugitive."

"Only a semi-fugitive," she corrects. "You're under restricted liberty."

"So you're okay with that?"

"I'm in this now. You go, I go. I'll finish getting ready. You get us some airline tickets."

"Umm, yeah ... about that ..."

"What?" she says. "What about that?"

"I kind of put up a fuss on the phone when Fogle told me not to leave town."

"How much of a fuss?"

"Enough of a fuss that I imagine the next thing he did was call security at the airport and told them not to let me fly out of here."

"Shit. Are you sure?"

"No, but I'm sure enough that if we risked it, we'd probably find ourselves in real custody. So it's you and me with the wind blowing through our hair again, I think."

She shoots me a quick suspicious glance. "This isn't just a ploy to keep from flying, is it? So you can have your way?"

"No, I swear. I was all geared up for a window seat and a little bag of peanuts. The whole works."

"All right, because if I find out you play little passive-aggressive mind games, I'm going to be very disappointed in you."

Within fifteen minutes, we are both ready to go. Fortunately, the hotel has brown-bag breakfasts in the lobby for business travelers in a hurry, and that's us. We grab two and head to the parking garage to get the Sebring. Rebecca offers to take the first driving shift, and I instruct her on how to get onto the interstate northbound. We have a very long day ahead, and we both know it.

As the miles pass, a thought comes to her and she says to me, "This may be a stupid question, but when you get these messages, these assignments, they give you all this information—who it's for, where they are, how to get there. Wouldn't it make more sense just to give you a phone number, so you can call them and warn them, instead of doing all this traveling?"

"Not a stupid question at all," I reply. "And an idea that I had too, early on. I tried it once. But imagine this: You're at work last week, and you get a phone call from a man you've never met, someone whose name is unfamiliar, whose voice you don't recognize. He tells you to quit your job, pack your things, leave Key West immediately, and go back home to Ohio. What would you think?"

"Psyyyy-cho," she answers.

"Exactly. A voice on the telephone is quick, but it carries no weight, even if I claim to be someone the person knows. Think about it: What was it about my message to you that held the most weight?"

"The fact that you showed up there. That you drove 1,200 miles to give that message to someone you'd never met."

"There you go. This is why I have to be there. Why they have to look at my eyes and hear my words and choose to believe me or not, with me standing there in front of them."

"So … what happened to the one you tried to call on the phone?"

It takes me several very pained seconds of looking away as I search for the right words to say. In the end, all I can come up with is "Nothing good." It ends the conversation in a hurry.

For about an hour, the radio is the only sound we share. The memory of past failures still stings, and she realizes that she has touched a nerve. I didn't mean to make her feel bad, but there is no easy way to dismiss what transpired without inviting more conversation about the past, and neither one of us is ready for that right now.

After that silent hour, she makes the decision to turn off the radio and change the subject to the matter at hand. "I keep thinking about Wyandotte, where we're going," she says. "I know I've heard the name before, which is strange, because you said it's been abandoned for years, right?"

"*Almost* abandoned," I specify. "Most of the people left there eighteen years ago. A number of families stayed for a while, but it got to be too much for them and they left too. Now only one family is left there."

"What drove everybody away? You mentioned a natural disaster. Was it a fire, an earthquake?"

"I don't know," I tell her. "Usually, I'm given exactly as much information as I need to find my subject and convince them that what I have to tell them is true."

"Who's your subject this time?"

"Mr. and Mrs. William Harbison," I reply.

"And their house is going to collapse?"

"So I'm told."

"God, that sucks. Well, maybe this will be the incentive they need to finally move out of town, just let it go."

"You think so?" I ask with a knowing smile. "Let me ask you something: Why would you live in a town all by yourself after everybody else moved out?"

She thinks about it. "I don't know. Maybe it was a family home for generations. Maybe they've got nowhere else to go."

"But you'd agree that their insistence on staying isn't just random or even casual, right? Something's keeping them there."

"Yeah, I guess so."

"So you see we may have a difficult task on our hands."

Hour follows hour, and Rebecca's first shift at the wheel ends, giving me a chance to drive again. I catch her looking over at me from time to time as I'm driving, but she's remaining curiously quiet, especially given the look on her face. Eventually, as I make my way onto Interstate 77, I have to know. "What's that look?"

She plays it very innocent. "What look?"

"The look you've been giving me for about ten minutes, every time you think I'm not looking at you. That sort of knowing half-smile."

"Can't a girl look at a guy?"

"Sure. But there seems to be something behind that look. Something you want to say, maybe?"

"I was just remembering last night," she says. "The good parts, I mean."

"They *were* good."

She reaches over and takes my hand in hers. I make no effort to resist. "I guess I just wanted to thank you for being with me that way."

"Well, you're welcome. It was something I wanted too. I just … couldn't be the one to ask."

"That's why I asked. Your hesitance caught me by surprise. It was …"

"Please don't say 'refreshing,'" I interrupt. "I'm not sure I'd know what to do with refreshing."

"Then how about surprising?" she asks. "Because that's what it was. Guys aren't supposed to be hesitant. They're supposed to be sex-crazed animals who don't give a damn about the girl's feelings or needs."

Her words sadden me. "Is this what you're used to?"

She nods. "Too often, yeah. But that wasn't you. From the start, you were so focused on me, on what I wanted and needed. Where did that come from?"

"I don't know. Just who I am, I suppose."

"Well, it took me by surprise, and I liked it. I don't know why, but I didn't expect it from you." She hesitates a moment, then voices a question. "Tristan … last night wasn't your first time, was it?"

I give an embarrassed laugh. "No, it wasn't my first time. As romantic as that scenario is, I'm sorry to say that my chastity is long since compromised. Why would you think it was my first time? Was I that bad?"

"Oh, hell no. Far from it. There was just something in your manner—the respect you showed me. It …" Then it hits her, and a new look of wonder lights her face. "Oh my God …" she says quietly.

"What?"

"I just realized what it really is."

"What are you talking about?"

"You've never had sex before with someone you didn't love."

I search for words to dismiss the idea, but they don't come. I want to deny it and I don't even know why. It feels like an accusation, though I know that's not what she intends. "No. I haven't."

My face falls, maybe with embarrassment, I'm not sure. But she sees it and tries at once to reconcile. "Tristan, you don't have to feel defensive or anything like that. I just … didn't know, and didn't expect that to be the case. It's just one of many pleasant surprises I'm finding out about you in this time together. I didn't mean to force a confession out of you."

"It's okay," I tell her, half meaning it. "I just didn't think it'd be that obvious."

"It's not obvious. I figured it out because I'm getting to know you. And I like the things I'm learning. The reason I had sex with you …" She corrects herself. "The reason I made love with you last night is because there's something good and powerful in you that speaks to me. It makes me want to be near you. It makes me want to stay with you on this errand we're on. I just hope I didn't seduce you into compromising your principles by being intimate with me."

"Rebecca, it's … it's not like that. You didn't get me drunk and take advantage of me when I was passed out. I knew what I was doing. But now, knowing what you know about me, I don't want you to be overwhelmed by what it all might mean."

She nods in understanding. "That's the thing. I'm still not sure what it all might mean. In case you haven't noticed, we're kind of making up the rules as we go along. I don't know what's going to happen tomorrow, or—hell—even today. For all we know, that house might fall on us too."

"I won't let that happen," I say vehemently.

"That's very kind and very noble of you, but let's not get too far ahead of ourselves. We still have a lot of hours of driving, and then a lot to do in Pennsylvania, I suspect."

"Probably."

"What are you going to do if they don't believe you?"

"Try my best to convince them, I guess. And if that doesn't work, when the time comes, I'll grab the husband and you grab the wife, and we'll physically drag them out of that house before it falls on top of them."

Rebecca looks amazed at the forthrightness of my suggestion. "Jesus, can we do that?"

"Wouldn't be the first time."

"But isn't that … I don't know … altering history or something?"

"You watch too many movies," I tell her. "This is why I'm there, to alter history before it happens. Okay, I'll grant you that if I ever go back in time and change something, *then* I've probably broken the rules. But barring that, I think we're okay." I see an uneasy look on her face. "What's the matter? Not up for manhandling anybody today?"

"I just wasn't expecting it. I can manhandle. Pinned *you* pretty good last night," she reminds me.

"That you did."

As morning turns to afternoon, I become aware of the blue Honda sedan. It has been in the lane behind me for several miles, staying about four car lengths back, and staying in whichever lane I choose. I can see a single figure in the car, most likely male, but can't get a good look at him. I keep an eye on him without being too obvious about it; I don't want to worry Rebecca. Under ordinary circumstances, I would think nothing of it, but with everything that's happened in the past three days, nothing is ordinary. I need to lose him without causing a fuss.

"You getting hungry?" I ask Rebecca casually.

"Yeah, I could eat," she replies. "Drive-thru?"

"No, we're making good time. There are some restaurants at the next exit. Let's pick one and sit down like civilized people. What do you say?"

"I have no objection to civilized."

"Great."

I get off at the next exit without signaling. A check of my rearview mirror makes my heart speed up. The blue Honda is getting off as well. *Man, it sucks being right sometimes.* I still don't want to worry Rebecca. I'll proceed as planned to a restaurant, and if there's going to be a confrontation, it'll be out in the open.

I turn right, and as expected, the Honda turns right after me. "Any preference about where we go?" I ask.

"You pick," she says. "I picked yesterday."

I continue for about four blocks, giving the Honda a chance to prove me wrong by stopping at a gas station. He doesn't; he just keeps going, either unaware or utterly unconcerned that I'm on to him. I stifle any fear I'm feeling and choose a destination—a Denny's on the left side of the road. I signal this time and get into the left-turn lane, discreetly watching the driver of the Honda do the same thing. It is to be an epic showdown at Denny's; not the stuff of legend, but it'll do.

I choose a parking spot near the building and brace myself mentally for what's to come. At this point, I can't keep Rebecca in the dark anymore. "We may have trouble," I say to her quietly.

Worry overtakes her expression. "What? What's going on?"

"I'm not sure yet. I'm going to take care of it. Whatever happens, I want you to stay safe. Come on, let's go."

She looks like she has a thousand questions, but there's no time. We put the top up, get out of the car, and lock it. By now, the Honda is parked and its driver has gotten out as well. I don't recognize him. White male, thirties or forties, dressed kind of business casual. I don't see an obvious weapon on him, but all I can do is watch him out of the corner of my eye. It's time to make a decision. The restaurant is crowded; there are families inside. Forcing this confrontation in there could be dangerous. It'll have to be outside, but in view of the building, in view of the road. I'll go almost as far as the door. *It's time. It's time. It's time.*

We step away from the Sebring and make our way to the building entrance. Rebecca is just in front of me. She gets to the door and opens it for me, but I hesitate. Our pursuer is just a few steps behind, and it's time to let him catch up. It has to be quick, and it has to be now.

Everything happens in a flash, a blur of motion. The man is a single step behind me now, and I turn. With coordination I didn't realize I have, I grab him by the lapels of his shirt and push him hard against the brick wall just to the left of the glass doors to the restaurant. He is taken by surprise and doesn't have time to put up a fight. His body hits the wall, and I am instantly in his face, demanding, "What do you think you're doing?"

His answer is amazingly calm, given the circumstances. "Minding my own business. You should try it."

I don't share his calm as I continue my interrogation, to the horror of Rebecca, who can only look on in stunned silence. "Cut the shit. I know you've been following us for miles. Why? What do you want?"

Now growing tired of this, he moves swiftly, grabbing my wrists in a flash and holding them tightly. He makes no move away from the wall, but I realize to my embarrassment and fear that he is now control of the altercation. "I want lunch," he says, still with that aggravating aplomb. "You're the ones in the convertible?"

"That's right. You followed behind us, you got off where we got off, and now you're here. I want answers!"

"I was using you as bear bait."

In response to my confused look, he explains, "You were driving fifteen over the limit, so I figured you had a radar detector. I wanted to speed without getting caught, so I paced you. Then I felt like lunch, so I came here."

"So … you're not following us?"

"No."

"So I just assaulted an innocent person?"

"Yeah, pretty much."

I have to ask. "How can you be so calm about it?"

"Buddy, I'm a bail bondsman. First thing they teach us is to keep your head when a crazy person comes at you."

"Yeah, about that …"

"So I figured I'd hear what you had to say, and then rip your heart out if it needed ripping out." He releases my wrists and I take a step back.

"Look, I'm really sorry. I …" I pull twenty dollars out of my pocket. "Let me at least buy you lunch."

"Okay." He takes the twenty from me. "I think you'll understand if I ask you and your friend to eat somewhere else."

"Of course. Again, I'm very sorry. I overreacted, and I'm very grateful to you for being so forgiving, and not … doing the heart-ripping thing you talked about."

"Look, pal, I don't know what trouble you're in, and I don't want to know. I've been in this business a lot of years, and I've seen some shit. You can imagine. I know that things aren't always what they look like. Just don't be too quick to jump on somebody because you think he's your enemy. And don't be too quick to trust somebody because you think he's your friend. All right?"

"Thank you," I say humbly.

"You folks be careful." He looks over at Rebecca, giving her a look that seems to me to say *especially you*. She smiles apologetically at him as he enters the restaurant. At this point, I am aware that patrons inside the Denny's are looking at me. It's time to leave here. I get back in the car, and Rebecca follows silently. Without a word spoken, I start the car and get us out of this town, back onto the interstate, heading north.

Five full minutes pass with both of us staring ahead at the road, neither able to speak a word to start the very necessary conversation.

Finally, she finds the words and the courage, and a question emerges, quietly and without accusation. "What happened back there?"

I am ashamed, so ashamed I can barely speak of it. Though she saw every moment of it, I still want to hide it from her, pretend it didn't happen, anything. "I made a mistake," is all I can say.

"You thought he was following us?" she asks. I nod. "So why did you want to confront him like that? He could have killed you."

"I know that now. But back there, all I could think was that he could have killed *you,* and I couldn't let him do that."

"You were ready to risk your own life for mine? Why? Why would you do that?"

"I don't … Please don't make me answer that, because I don't have an answer. I just knew I had to protect you."

"Tristan, I don't want you getting hurt over me. Please promise me you won't take risks like that again."

I look at her face, see the insistence there. I can barely make eye contact. "I don't know if I can promise you that."

"Well, you have to. Because if you don't, I'm gonna make you pull over right here, and I'll hitchhike the rest of the way to Ohio. *Promise me.*"

"I promise," I say quietly.

In the minutes that pass, we both try to regain our calm, find our composure. "I'm still hungry," she says. "If you want to get off at the next exit, we can get that lunch we both wanted."

In northern Virginia, several miles further up the road, we get off the highway, this time without accompaniment, and find a sit-down family restaurant where we can have some lunch. By now, the initial shame of the recent altercation is starting to ebb in me, slowly earning a place in my memory as something I'll regret for the rest of my life. The thing that will stay with me the most is the man's unwavering calm. He stood there patiently while a stranger accosted him in front of Denny's. Sure, he's a bail bondsman, so I'm certain this isn't the first time he's been threatened. And I imagine on the sliding scale between genuine threat and complete pussy, I fall closer to the latter than the former.

But Rebecca was right—he could have killed me, and it would have been self-defense. I got so caught up in the self-imposed role of being white knight and protector that I completely disregarded my own safety, which in turn would have jeopardized hers too. But what else could I do? If this man had been a legitimate threat to us, there's no telling what he might have done.

I have to ask myself at this point, am I being this protective of her because of the message I was tasked to deliver to her or am I being this protective of her because I'm falling for her? I have no good answer; in fact, I'm not even convinced that I *am* falling for her. What she said earlier about my sexual history was right on the money. For me, sex always followed love. But not last night; I was willing to put aside my principles and just *feel*. Still, the feelings were so strong and the bond that emerged between us was so powerful that it makes me wonder if I really am falling for her.

And if I am, what then? Barring anything earth-shaking today, we will be in Ohio tomorrow, and I'll have to drop her off, let her get back to school. Much as I would like to stay with her, I don't suspect the assignments will stop, so I'll be on the road again. Still, I can't regret the intimacy we shared last night. It was like nothing I've ever experienced before.

It is at this moment that I leave my own thoughts and become aware of my surroundings, realizing to my dismay that I have been sitting at the table with a fork in my hand and my mouth slightly ajar for several minutes while I had this internal argument with myself. Rebecca, ever the model of tact and discretion, is doing the wave-your-hand-in-front-of-the-eyes-of-the-catatonic-person-to-see-if-anyone's-home gesture. A few nearby diners are watching in quiet amusement.

She smiles when at last I return. "Welcome back," she says pleasantly. "You … uh … checked out for a little bit there. I thought you might be getting another message from the spirit world, but you weren't writhing in pain, so I figured something else might be up. Care to share?"

"Sorry. Just got a little lost in my own thoughts."

"A little? That's an understatement. I was this close to writing something funny on your forehead." Her thumb and forefinger held very close together indicate just how imminent my defacement was.

"I thank you for your forbearance."

She downs a breaded mushroom. "What are friends for? So what's got you so deep in thought?"

I look at my plate. *Chicken pot pie? Did I order this?* "The whole Denny's thing. It's got me thinking too much. I've been in potentially dangerous situations before, since this whole thing started two years ago, but then it was just me. With you along, it changes everything."

"I'm sorry," she says. "After tomorrow, that won't be a problem."

"No, I didn't mean it like that. You have nothing to be sorry about. I'm glad you're with me. I just can't take chances like I have been."

"Would it help if I told you I'm grateful to you for protecting me?"

"I suppose."

"Would it also help if I told you I'm a big girl and I've done a pretty good job of taking care of myself so far?"

"I suppose."

She reaches out and touches my hand, inviting me to look her in the eyes. "Tristan, it's okay. We'll get through this. We'll help that family in Wyandotte, and then we'll get me to Ohio."

"Any idea what happens then?" I ask her. "Where will you stay?"

"With my father. He's closer to the campus. And my mother and I haven't gotten along well for years."

"How will your father feel about you coming home again?"

"I don't know. It's been a long time. Once I get enrolled again, I'll live on campus, so I won't see much of him. I kind of think that's the way he'd want it."

"Am I dropping you off in the middle of a bad situation?"

She hesitates before answering. "I really don't know. Things between me and my father have never been what you would call warm."

"You're not going to be in any danger there, are you?"

"No no, it's nothing like that. I'm still his little girl. It's just going to take some re-adjustment for a while."

After lunch, we get right back in the car, put the top down again, and make the commitment to get to our destination. We are still almost five hours away and we have a little more than seven hours before the Harbisons' house, hopes, and dreams are all going to come crashing down.

We're able to continue at fifteen miles per hour over the speed limit. With little need for stops or breaks, we make good time, passing through Virginia into West Virginia, then into Pennsylvania. Conversation trickles down to a minimum, as we allow the radio to do the talking for us. I can't be sure what she's thinking about, although a few obvious topics come to mind. As for me, I'm doing what I usually do before an assignment: rehearsing what I'm going to say and how I'm going to say it. *Dear strangers, you don't know me, but I'm here to turn your world upside down. I know this sounds crazy, but if you don't do exactly what I'm about to tell you, horrible horrible things are going to happen. They're not my fault, so please don't kill the messenger, and if it's not too much trouble, please don't ask me how I know all of this, because I don't have a good answer, even after all this time.*

The words never come out that way, of course. I always present them with compassion and sympathy, well aware that circumstances drastic enough to warrant my arrival require tact and a soft tone. I often wonder how I would react if the situation was reversed, if I was on the receiving end of such news.

"There, exit 26." Rebecca's words snap me out of my thoughts and bring me back into the moment. "This is our exit."

The sign points to a state highway and two towns, one east of us and the other west. I notice that Wyandotte is not on the sign; abandoned towns don't warrant signage, I suppose.

"That means we're six miles from Wyandotte," I say.

"And it's 5:10. What time is the house coming down?"

"Not until 7:46. We made very good time. Do you need to stop for anything?"

"No," she replies. "Let's just get there. The more time we have with these people, the better we'll be."

I take the exit and head west, based on the directions in my head. The state highway is lightly traveled and mostly nondescript. There are a few businesses here and there, the occasional shack or mobile home, and a lot of trees. Five miles later, we come to the intersection of another state highway. It is the road into Wyandotte, and still no sign is there to inform us of this. I've been to ghost towns in Colorado, places abandoned for 100 years or more, and each one has been marked with signs directing the curious to come and explore. No such welcome exists for Wyandotte; it's almost as if someone—or everyone—wanted the place forgotten. The thought disturbs me as I make the right turn, the final mile toward Wyandotte, Pennsylvania and the task of telling William and Virginia Harbison that their lives are about to change forever.

Chapter 10

"You doing all right?" Rebecca asks as we make our way toward the town.

"A little edgy; the usual. How about you?"

"A little bit, yeah," she admits. "But mostly okay."

Any signs of life that were apparent on the feeder highway are gone now on the road to Wyandotte. We see a few boarded-up stores as we approach. Grass grows wild and unkempt. Weeds own the landscape. At last, we reach the edge of town, where we see an old wooden signpost bearing the carefully carved and painted words "Welcome to Wyandotte. Our pride, our home." The sign is decades old and has fallen into such disrepair that it looks as if it is about to fall over at any moment. The state's green sign with the town name and population is gone, the final confirmation of the place's demise.

On long-deserted buildings, graffiti tells the tale of those who have passed through: Wes & Kelli '93. Steelers rule. TC + RL 4-eva. Class of 2005. Then, on the road ahead, we see large words spray painted on cracked and pitted asphalt, words that send a chill through me: Welcome to hell.

Rebecca sees it too and her expression falls. "Tristan …"

"I know. I see it."

"I don't want to be in hell. Why is it hell?"

"I guess somebody didn't enjoy their stay."

"This is starting to creep me out. Where's their house?"

"On the 200 block of Spring Street," I reply.

Without even pausing to think about it, she says, "Turn right at the park up here." I am astonished by her words, and looking over at her, I realize that she is as well.

"Now how would you know that?" I ask her, making the right turn.

"I don't know," she replies honestly. "I just know that this is where Spring Street would be. Do you think some of your abilities are rubbing off on me?"

"Anything's possible. But it would be a first."

The streets of Wyandotte do indeed paint a hellish picture. Every house is abandoned, many of them dilapidated, ransacked, crumbling. Some have been lost to fire. Children's toys litter the sidewalks, broken, rusted, worn away by years of disuse. The streets themselves are in need of repair that will never come. Cracks and potholes and discarded items make an obstacle course that keeps me on my guard as we approach the Harbisons' house. Then, up ahead, I see it—the only occupied home in the entire town. It is by no means elegant, but compared to everything around it, the one-story home is an oasis. It looks cared for. Signs at the perimeter politely warn trespassers away. As we park at the curb, I only hope that the homeowners will view us as visitors and not trespassers.

I put the top up and we get out of the car, looking for signs of the inhabitants. There is a car in their driveway, an older-model Ford, which I hope is a good sign. As we are making our way up the driveway (calmly and with no sudden moves), the front door to the house opens and a man in his early sixties steps out. "You folks lost?" he calls to us.

"No, sir," I reply. "Are you Mr. Harbison, by chance?"

"I don't know if chance has anything to do with it," he says, "but I'm William Harbison. Do I know you?"

"I can't imagine you do. My name is Tristan, and this is Rebecca." There's no need for pretense or masquerade this time. "We've driven here from Atlanta because we were asked to deliver a message to you."

"That's an awful long way to deliver a message. We do have a telephone, you know."

Rebecca shoots me a quick *told-ya-so* glance, and it elicits a smile from me. "I was asked to deliver the message to you and Mrs.

Harbison in person. Would you mind if we came inside for a couple of minutes?"

He assesses us visually, deciding whether our story checks out and whether we look dangerous. Apparently he believes that it does, and we don't, because he opens the door for us and says, "Come on in."

The interior of the house has the same no-nonsense, no-frills quality as its exterior. It is home to this couple, who do not have to worry about neighbors, relatives, or even casual visitors—except today. The Harbisons are tidy without being fastidious, and they have a love of books, Hummel figurines, and religious décor. As I look around the living room, I try very hard not to picture everything in ruin in two hours' time.

Mrs. Harbison meets us in the living room. "Hello," she says, apparently quite surprised to have people calling. Part of living in a ghost town, I guess. "I'm Virginia."

"I'm Tristan, ma'am," I reply, "and this is Rebecca."

"Ginny, these young people have come here from Atlanta. They have a message to give us."

"Won't you have a seat?" she says. "I've made iced tea. Would you like some?"

"That'd be great," Rebecca says, and I nod in agreement. Inside, though, I am tied in knots over what I have to tell these people. On the journey, it's a concept, words to be spoken, but once I meet the recipient, put a face to the name, it complicates things beyond measure.

Ginny Harbison brings us each a glass of tea and then joins her husband on the couch. Rebecca sits on a wing chair, facing them. I choose to stand; it's easier to fidget that way. *God, I hate this part.* "Mr. and Mrs. Harbison, what I'm about to tell you might be hard to believe but it's very important that you understand two things: First, what I have to tell you is entirely true. And second, I swear to you that we mean you no harm. We're here to help you."

The couple look at each other warily. "Son," Mr. Harbison says, "if that's the warm-up, I don't think I'm looking forward to hearing the pitch. You'd best say what you came here to say."

I pause long enough to take a breath. "At 7:46 tonight, there's going to be an accident. Important structural components of your house will fail, and the house is going to collapse. I'm very sorry."

Mrs. Harbison stands in disbelief, her face riddled with shock and fear. Her husband, interestingly enough, receives the news with resolute calm. "That can't be!" she cries out. "That's not possible! Why would you say such a thing?"

Mr. Harbison puts a calming hand on her shoulder. "Ginny, be calm. It's going to be all right. We'll get through this."

I look directly at him. "Then you do believe me?"

He nods. "I've seen the bowing of the joists for about a year now. I've suspected that the support beams were rotting, but I couldn't get behind the drywall to see them."

"You knew?" Ginny asks, astonished. "Why didn't you tell me?"

"I didn't want to worry you, Mother," he says to his wife. "Not until I could be sure. Besides, we don't have the money to fix it, even if contractors would come out here."

She is near tears. "William, what are we going to do?"

"We can help you," Rebecca chimes in, standing. "We have two hours. That'll give us time to get things out of the house—heirlooms, anything that's irreplaceable. As many of your possessions as we can carry to safety."

"That's very kind of you," William says. "I accept your offer. We should probably get to it then, since time is short. You're sure about that time, 7:46?"

"Very sure," I answer.

"All right then. Wouldn't want to find myself buried under rubble at 7:15."

And so the race to clear the house begins. With no storage shed and no trailer truck available, our goal is to get as many possessions as possible into the front yard until the Harbisons can figure out what to do and where to go. I silently wish that they would consider their large collection of books to be replaceable, but no such luck. I quickly find myself boxing up books and carting the ferociously heavy boxes out to the lawn, one after the other. Ginny Harbison concentrates on the Hummels and religious figurines first, while William brings out album after album of photographs, some containing old newspaper articles. Rebecca carries out electronics—their TV, radio, small appliances.

"We'll need to turn off the power to the house before 7:46," I tell the group. "We don't want a fire on top of everything else."

As the unloading continues, Rebecca asks, "How did all of this happen?"

"It's an old house," William replies. "Over time, the support beams have started to give out. I've called contractors to come and look at the house, but none of them want to come out here. So I prayed that God would send me a warning if something bad was going to happen. Then the two of you arrived."

Rebecca and I look at each other upon hearing this, each pondering the implications of what it means. But there is little time for pondering, with many more objects to be transported outside.

"Actually, I was talking about the town," Rebecca tells him. "Why did everyone leave?"

This time, the Harbisons exchange a glance, one of surprise, based on the looks on their faces. "You mean you don't know about the smog?" Ginny Harbison asks.

Rebecca shakes her head. Those words have an ominous quality to them: *the smog.* I've been through smog before, but bad enough to clear out an entire town?

"I'll tell you," William says, "but we have to keep working." We agree, and he begins his tale. "It was eighteen years ago April. It was a bit warmer than usual, and then a cold front came through, bringing very heavy cloud cover over Wyandotte. You may have noticed we're in a valley here; that does strange things with the weather sometimes. It certainly did that day. Take a look over here. You see that building on the hill?"

He points to a huge factory about a mile away, towering over the town on a short hill. "Allegheny Zinc Works," he continues. "For decades, they were the reason this town existed. They pulled zinc out of the ground and processed and shipped it all over the world. At any given time, half the adult population of this town worked for Allegheny. They were good to the community, doing charitable work, keeping Wyandotte in good condition. They even sponsored a Christmas parade each year."

As he says this, I happen to be looking in Rebecca's direction, and I see her with a far-off expression on her face. At the exact moment the three words escape William Harbison's mouth, I see Rebecca mouthing them too: *a Christmas parade*. But before I can ask her about it, he is continuing with his story.

"For a long time, this was a portrait of industrial small-town America worthy of a Norman Rockwell calendar."

"Until ..." I prompt.

William nods. "Until. April 22, those clouds rolled in and stayed there over the town. So thick, the sun could barely get through. The weather people call it an inversion. What's supposed to go up stays down, and what's supposed to stay down goes up. At first, the people went about their business and didn't think anything of it. We get bad weather from time to time, and it was just cloudy and cool; no rain or storms. So the kids went to school, the adults went to their jobs, and the factory kept on working around the clock, just like they always did.

"Night fell, and everything still seemed normal. But the next day, when daylight was supposed to come, it didn't. The clouds were still there, but now there was something else with them, something dark and thick and acrid, like soot or smoke. Well, people kept going about their business that day, but things started to change. People were getting sick. Older folks and children at first, but as the day wore on, healthy adults were coughing too. By nightfall on the twenty-third, we knew there was a serious problem. People's pets were dying. Then a couple of the oldest residents, and an infant. That brought people in from Pittsburgh, scientists with devices for testing the air quality. They found fluorine gas and sulfur dioxide in the air. These things came out of Allegheny's smokestacks all the time, but usually they drifted up into the sky and away from us. But those clouds trapped the emissions at ground level, right where people were breathing them."

"Didn't somebody notify the factory?" Rebecca asks.

"Yes, they did. On the evening of the twenty-third, the scientists went with two local doctors to talk to the plant manager and report their findings. They said that the only way to protect the people was to shut the plant down until the clouds passed. The problem is, a zinc factory isn't like a lamp or a TV set. You can't just flip the switch and be done with it. The zinc is processed at temperatures of 900 to 1,600 degrees. Shutting down the plant would leave tons and tons of it useless and create workflow problems throughout the factory. The place had never been completely shut down in more than sixty years. The managers were sympathetic to the problem, but they refused to do the shutdown."

William pauses briefly to go in and retrieve more items from the house. Little by little, we are managing to salvage a lifetime of treasures. Rebecca and I stick close to him as he tells his story, not wanting to miss a detail.

"So what happened then?" I ask.

"Morning came again, just as dark as the day before. Those clouds refused to move, and the factory refused to shut down operations. By now, some folks weren't taking any chances. They were staying in their homes, keeping all their doors and windows shut. Those who went outside wore masks or handkerchiefs over their nose and mouth. And inside of a few minutes, those clean whites they wore were stained black from the air itself. The local hospitals were filling up with Wyandotte's residents, and word began to come back that more people were dying. The mayor stepped in and got a court order, demanding that Allegheny Zinc Works shut down the plant until such time as the inversion cleared. Now they had no choice. They did what it took and shut down operations.

"But by then, the damage was done. By the time those clouds passed two days later, twenty-three people were dead. Four thousand got sick. We lost hundreds of animals—cats, dogs, chickens. All this in a town of 14,000 people. It was like nothing anyone had ever seen before. All the vegetation within a half mile of the factory was killed. When the clouds passed and people were able to go outside again, we thought it was over, but it wasn't. Those poisons got into the soil, into the water table, and they stayed. It affected everything in town.

"Hundreds of people moved away within the first two months after the smog. They couldn't bear to be near this town anymore. Allegheny Zinc never rebounded either. They shut down that same year, and the exodus continued. Within a year, there were only a thousand people living here. Within two years, it was down to a hundred. Five years after the smog, only three families remained. Now it's just Ginny and me."

Rebecca is hanging on his every word, looking astonished at the tale. "What will you do now?" she asks. "Will you leave Wyandotte?"

It is Ginny who answers. "We're not leaving here. Wyandotte is our home. Everyone else left, put it behind them, tried to forget that this place ever existed. We're its last defenders. We've kept up the park and the cemetery, kept the church in good order. We've seen this town through sickness and health, and we can't leave now, not even if this house falls to the ground."

I look at my watch—6:55. Less than an hour until it does just that. Fortunately, we're making good progress. But one question remains. "Where will you live?" I ask them.

"Two blocks away," William replies, "is the Pruett house. It's been abandoned for years, but Sanford Pruett left me the keys. I've used it for years for storage, kept it locked against looters and vandals. It's livable. We can bring our things over there little by little and make that our new home. It'll be different, but at least we're not giving up on Wyandotte."

Rebecca decides to ask a question at this point, one I would have avoided. "Did you lose anyone in the smog?"

Ginny works hard to stifle tears upon hearing the question, but she is visibly shaken by it, and turns away from us to compose herself. William provides the answer. "Our son Joshua. He was eleven years old. He went to school during the smog. Said he didn't want to miss two days of classes. We kept him inside after school, but by then the damage was done."

"Oh my God, I'm so sorry. Did Allegheny compensate you for your loss?"

"What they did wasn't compensation," William says. "It was an insult. They did to us what they did to everybody who lost family in the smog. Paid for the burial, then had their lawyers make us sign something absolving the company of all blame. It tore me up, signing that. But they said if we didn't, we'd get nothing at all."

"That's terrible."

"It's in the past," he says. "We can't change the things that were."

"When we're done unloading," I say, "we'll help you drive things over to the Pruett house. We'll bring things in there with you."

"Thank you," William says, "and God bless you both. I know I'll be very sad when this house dies, but your kindness has softened the blow today."

We continue working, getting as much furniture as we can out of the house. It's tiring work and the heavier pieces are taking their toll. Then there'll be the fun of putting it all back in the new house. But it's a small price to pay. These people are truly alone out here, and their words have brought me closer than anyone ever has to understanding why I'm on the mission I'm on. Maybe God did send me. I've never been terribly religious, but I've always believed. How could there not be something controlling all of this? The world is too magnificent and terrible to be the product of random chance.

At 7:12 PM, the house emits a loud creaking sound; the collapse is not early, but it is coming, there is no doubt. It motivates us to step up our efforts, move faster, and get as much out of there as we can. We load boxes into the Harbisons' car, and he drives them over to the house that will soon be their home. By nightfall, they should have enough of their possessions in place to spend the night there.

I finally find a moment to take Rebecca aside. "What's going on?" I ask her.

"What do you mean?"

"Something's changed. Earlier, you knew where Spring Street was, and then, when William was talking about Allegheny's Christmas parade, I saw you … it's like you knew about it, or like you remembered it."

"I feel like I've been here before. I can't explain it, but when he talked about that Christmas parade, it stirred a memory in me from a long time ago. Maybe it wasn't the Christmas parade here, but I know I've been to one when I was little. I want to do everything we can to help these people."

"I appreciate that, but you can't get attached. We're here to deliver the message, which we did. We stayed on to help them; that was our choice, but it's not required of us. We can't allow ourselves to get mixed up in their lives."

She immediately gives me a disapproving glance, in time for me to realize how hypocritical those words sound. "I know what you're going to say, and my answer is 'do what I say, not what I do.' They can't come with us."

"I know."
"Car's crowded enough as it is."
"Uh huh."
"Shouldn't you be lifting things?"

At 7:38, we are all gathered in the front yard. Everything that can realistically be removed from the house has been removed. Most of it is on the Harbisons' lawn, looking like the world's most comprehensive yard sale. A few dozen boxes are already at the Pruett house which, from my brief stop inside, looks pleasant enough. It will provide shelter for them, but how much of a home it will feel like remains to be seen. Moving with two hours' notice isn't exactly conducive to inviting people to put their feet up and feel right at home.

The electricity has been shut off, such as it is. With no utility company in town, the pair has been living off the grid, using generators to provide their modest electrical needs. Their only phone service is via cellular, which will travel easily to the new house with them. Before the refrigerator is turned off, Ginny makes us sandwiches, which are very welcome after all the work we've put in. Once they're gone and the magnitude of the work stands before us, the four of us are left in silence, as twilight begins to creep over the valley. No one is quite sure what to say or whether it is now time to leave. We've done everything we can for them, but it feels like leaving now would be akin to abandoning them.

"I want to go in one last time," William says quietly at 7:42.

"It's not safe," I tell him. "The time is too tight. We can't risk you getting caught inside when it happens."

"Then would you join us in a prayer?" he asks.

"We'd be honored to," Rebecca answers.

We form a circle on the front lawn, we four who have shared this experience. I hope that no one asks me to say a few words, because when it comes to things religious, I tend to get tongue-tied. Fortunately, William steps up to take care of it.

"Lord of hosts who watches over us every day, we thank you in this dark hour that you have seen fit to send two messengers to watch over us and aid us in our plight. Ours is not to question your wisdom or your ways. Ours is to love you and serve you and stand vigilantly over this, your fair Wyandotte. Thank you for the gift of steadfastness and longsuffering, to allow us to remain when all others have fled. Lord, we return this house to the earth from whence it came, and we thank you for letting it shelter us these many years, through storm and sun. We ask that you bless Tristan and Rebecca, and allow them long and healthy lives in which to do your bidding. All things in thy mercy. Amen."

"Amen," we respond together.

Seconds later, a sound emerges from within the house, a death groan of wood and nails and drywall and glass. Critical support beams in two rooms splinter and fail. Left to shoulder their burden as well, the beams in the other rooms quickly follow suit, and the little ranch house falls in on itself. Windows shatter and bookcases crumble. Large appliances are crushed under the weight of debris that seconds ago was a ceiling. Though I knew it was coming, it is still startling and very jarring. Rebecca flinches as each portion of the collapse occurs.

The destruction takes almost a full minute, as a chain reaction moves from room to room. I look at the aftermath and realize with no doubt that if the Harbisons had been inside, there is almost no chance that they would have survived.

Out on the lawn, William and Ginny watch their peaceful home's demise in stoic silence. Once it is done, Ginny begins to sob into William's shoulder. Though he is staunchly playing the role of the comforting husband, his eyes tell me that his heart is breaking, and that he would like nothing more than to weep with her for their loss, a loss that their God saw fit to warn them against but not to prevent.

Moved by it all, Rebecca comes to me and puts her arms around me as well, resting her face against my chest. "We did it," she says quietly, with a degree of satisfaction.

"Yes we did," I answer.

"You were great."

"Thanks. You were pretty great yourself."

The Harbisons take a moment to compose themselves, and then approach us. "There aren't words strong enough to thank you properly for what you've done," William says.

"You're alive and safe," I reply. "That's thanks enough."

"We don't have much money, but if there's a way I could repay you—even if it's just for the gas it took to get you here from Atlanta …"

I decline with a raised palm. "I couldn't, but thank you. For reasons I don't quite understand, this is what I do. God's given me enough money that I can focus on this and not worry about making ends meet."

"Then you're truly blessed," William says. "It's getting late, and you must be very tired. Will you consider spending the night with us as our guests?"

"That's very kind," I reply, "but we couldn't impose. You've got a lot of setting up to do in your new home, and the last thing you need is guests under foot, getting in the way. There are hotels at the last interstate exit we passed. We can spend the night in one of them before heading out in the morning. But thank you. You've been so thoughtful, even with everything you've been through today."

Ginny looks over at us. "What will the two of you do next?"

"You've caught Rebecca on her last mission," I answer. "Tomorrow she goes home, back to school and to her family."

"Then you're not married?" Ginny asks, surprised.

We both give a little laugh. "Not hardly," I say. "Actually, we've known each other all of three days. I delivered a message to her and then agreed to take her home to her family."

"Watching the two of you together," William comments, "we thought you were married. You work so well together. I never would have guessed you've known each other so short a time."

"It's been a very interesting three days," Rebecca says. "We've formed a very strong friendship in that time."

"What happens when you leave Rebecca at her home?" Ginny asks. "Will you ever see her again?"

All I can do is answer honestly. "We don't know. I certainly hope so, though. I'm very glad to know her. And I'm very glad we could help you tonight."

"I hope you don't think us foolish for wanting to stay here," William says.

"Not at all," I reply. "Your home is your home. I respect that."

"You're one of the few. Friends and family don't come here anymore. And it's not even out of fear. They've dismissed us as deluded and irrational. They believe we're clinging to a dead town. But Wyandotte could live again if people cared. Eighteen years ago, when Allegheny Zinc Works destroyed this town, the plant manager made a big speech to the people about finding new frontiers and looking towards the future. What he was really telling them was to run away, forget that Wyandotte ever existed, and bury the truth about what happened here. Everyone else may have done that, but we refuse to give Calvin Traeger that satisfaction."

My mind races. In the seconds that follow the utterance of that name, a thousand thoughts fill my head at once. Instantly, so much becomes clear. Above it all, one thought becomes paramount, and I have to find a way to convey it to my traveling companion. I am close enough to her that I hear the gasp escape her throat; fortunately, the Harbisons are too far away to hear. From the corner of my eye, I see her start to take a step forward, ready to pour forth her astonishment. Swiftly, I catch her wrist with my hand, stopping her forward progress. I turn to face her ever so briefly, just long enough to burn a look into her eyes that conveys an unquestionable command: *Say nothing.*

She sees the look and transfers the momentum of her step to something resembling a natural movement to be closer to me. I put my arm around her shoulder and try like hell to stifle back the anxiety in my voice. I feel my heart racing. "He was the one who made the decision to keep the plant open?" I ask.

"Yes. And for as long as I live, I'll hold him responsible for all those deaths."

I step over to this man who has lost so much, and I place a sympathetic hand on his shoulder. "I hope you can find forgiveness in your heart one day."

We hastily bid our goodbyes. It's clear to me that Rebecca can barely contain her anxiety, and every second we stay in the Harbisons' company is making it harder for her to hold her tongue. When at last we walk together to the Sebring, she whispers to me, fighting tears all the while, "Tristan …"

"I know," I whisper back. "But not here, not yet. Not while they can hear us."

I help her into the passenger's seat and quickly get behind the wheel, driving us a half mile to a park in the center of Wyandotte.

Once there, I park the car and look over at Rebecca. Neither of us can speak for many long, agonizing seconds. I have no words to begin this impossible conversation. She can't even make eye contact. Instead, her head is down, tucked tightly to her chest, her eyes squeezed shut to keep out the truth that's been revealed to her.

Just as I am finally contemplating the possibility of offering words of comfort, her tears explode forth from her in a primal shout of disbelief and rage. "No!" she sobs, emitting so many tears that I swear I can taste salt from across the car. "It's not true! It can't be true!"

"Rebecca …"

"He wouldn't do that, would he?"

"I don't know him," I say softly, in all honesty. "But you do. Did he manage a zinc factory?"

"He doesn't talk about that time in our lives," she says through her hitching sobs. "He doesn't talk about the past."

"You knew this town," I remind her. "Spring Street. The Christmas parade. You were three years old when it all happened. Young enough that memories are vague, but just old enough to be reminded when you see familiar sights again."

"No …" she says, her voice quivering with the realization that I could be right. She then lifts her head and looks out at the park where we have stopped. She glances from the fields to the benches, then over at the rusted, decaying remains of a playground. Suddenly, without warning, she opens her door and dashes from the car. I call to her but she does not even turn around. She runs, still crying, toward the playground equipment. Daylight is fading, and I don't want to lose sight of her, even for a minute, so I open my door and sprint after her.

My heart pains as I see her stop at the entrance to the playground and focus her attention on something, then drop to her knees and bury her head in her hands, sobbing uncontrollably.

From a distance, I can't tell what she's found that has her so upset. Moments later, I catch up to her and see that she is kneeling in front of a small engraved plaque, which now looks more like a tombstone than a dedication. There is barely enough light to read the words, but they tell me everything I need to know:

DEDICATED
TO THE PEOPLE OF
WYANDOTTE:
PERSEPHONE'S
PLAYLAND

A GIFT FROM
MR. AND MRS. CALVIN TRAEGER

She looks up at me with sorrow etched deep into her face, and utters two simple words that freeze my blood, words of terrified acceptance: "I'm home."

Chapter 11

Before I can reach out to comfort her, before I can even say a word of appeasement, Rebecca springs to her feet and runs back to the car, climbs in, and starts the engine. I hurry back and jump into the passenger's seat, fairly certain that if I dawdle, she will leave me behind.

"Rebecca, where are we going?"

She doesn't answer. At first, I am fearful that she wants to return to the Harbisons, to have words with them that would tell them who she is. I am relieved when her path takes us away from Spring Street, away from the factory, to the edge of town. Here, as everywhere else, there is no sign of life. The houses are bigger here, more elegant, or at least they were long ago, when they were inhabited. But this elegance has made them a prime target for vandals and looters, and their present level of violation makes me sad.

Rebecca proceeds like a woman possessed, tapping into memories long since buried, retracing streets that she must have only seen from the vantage point of a child's car seat. At this point, I don't even try to speak to her; I'm fairly convinced that she wouldn't hear me if I did. *I'm home,* she told me in that park. And that's precisely where she is going.

Two lefts and a right later, we are on a street called Fairview. At the end of a driveway—whose missing bricks suggest the smile of a gap-toothed child—sits the remains of a once-grand two-story Victorian home. The gate that long ago kept unwanted visitors at bay now stands mangled and useless. Rebecca turns on the brights and powers the Sebring up the driveway, not even flinching when the car's tires bounce and skip over the gaps left by missing bricks. At the end of the drive, she turns off the engine but leaves the halogen lights on, illuminating the double doors. Still wordless, she exits the car with haste and purpose, moving toward the house.

I open my door and step out. "Rebecca—"

Startled, she turns to look back at me, staring at my face as if she is actually surprised that I am there with her. "I'm home," she says again, in the tone of a powerless child. And without another word, she turns away from me and opens the door to the house.

Well aware of the potential danger, I run after her, catching up to her just inside the house. The light from the headlights does a good job of illuminating the exterior, but once inside, darkness owns the place, and I have to stop short just a few paces in, to keep from bumping into her.

"We can't stay here," I tell her gently. "It's too dark; it isn't safe."

She looks around, seeing the pervasive state of disarray that has consumed her childhood home. I can see only shapes in the darkness, silhouettes of debris. The smell of decay and mold fills my nostrils, burning its way into my throat and my lungs. I stifle a cough and put my hands firmly on her shoulders.

"Please come with me," I say. "I'll take us someplace where we can rest."

Her tears have stopped but she is nothing resembling herself. Gone is the strong, intelligent woman I've gotten to know over the past few days. Here, now in front of me is a frightened child whose entire life has been inverted in an instant. She looks at me, trying to find my expression in the darkness, just as I try to find hers. Silently, she gives in, allowing me to escort her out of the house.

Relief washes over me. I had visions of her running deeper into the house, maybe even up the stairs to try to find her old room. My mind conjures possible futures that include her falling through holes in the floor, being injured or even killed. I am powerfully relieved when she walks with me to safety.

Just a few steps from the car, we are back in the headlights' beam and I can see her face again. She is ashen, her eyes puffy from crying. I turn her to face me, knowing that she is not well, and she looks at me with no recognition in her eyes.

"What is it?" I ask her, very concerned.

A single word emerges in response. "The ..." Then her eyes roll back in her head and she loses consciousness, falling forward into my arms.

The fluorescent lights are very bright, particularly harsh in contrast to the darkness we faced in Wyandotte just a few hours ago. I've managed to filter out the sounds that have been all around me as I sit by Rebecca's bedside, but there's no way to block out that light. She is still unconscious, and I am feeling overpoweringly guilty. *I got her into this. She's here because of me. Tonight changed everything. How could I let myself get close to her like this when I know I have to let her go tomorrow?*

My ponderings are interrupted when I see her flutter her eyelids and open her eyes. She looks confused, disoriented until she sees me sitting by her bedside. "Where am I?" she asks weakly.

"Three Rivers Hospital. You fainted."

"That's impossible. I've never fainted in my life." Her voice is quiet, straining to form each sentence.

"All right then, you jumped into my arms and took a spontaneous three-hour nap."

"Three hours? I've been out for three hours?"

"Yes."

She lifts her arm, looking at the tube leading from it. "What's this?"

"I.V. fluids."

"Tristan, why am I in the hospital?"

"How much do you remember?" I ask her.

She thinks a moment. "Everything ... I think."

"When you came out of your house, you collapsed into my arms. Once I was sure you were breathing, I put you in the back seat and drove you to the nearest hospital. You're dehydrated and you have stress exhaustion. The doctor asked me where we'd been tonight, and I said Wyandotte. That prompted him to do some blood tests. You had some mold, asbestos, lead, and sulfur exposure too."

"Are *you* all right?" she asks.

"I'm not exactly ready to go out dancing, but I'd say I'm doing pretty well for an old man."

She smiles. I can see the weariness on her face. "How long do I have to stay here?"

"They want to keep you overnight for observation. There's two beds in this recovery room, and I made arrangements to sleep in the other one, so I'd be here if you need anything."

"It's not exactly the Hilton," she observes.

"Ironically enough, it's a bit more expensive than the Hilton. But the room service is better here."

"You think they'd let us have sex?" she quips.

"I think you've had enough fun for one day, tiger. But on the bright side, Detective Fogle called me a couple hours ago and said I was free to leave Atlanta."

"Lucky you. You wanna drive or should I?"

"I'll take us," I tell her with a smile. "I think you might oughta sleep."

"Yeah, I think so."

"If you need anything during the night, I want you to wake me or press the button to call the nurse, okay?"

I stand and go to her bedside. She reaches out a hand to me and I hold it in mine. "Tristan ... what am I going to do about my father?"

"I don't know. We can talk in the morning, after we've both had some sleep." I kiss her fingertips as I watch her struggle to stay awake long enough to talk to me.

"I'm scared," she says.

"I don't blame you. We learned some scary things today. Try to sleep, though."

"Don't leave me?"

"I wouldn't dream of it."

The night is uneventful for both of us, and morning arrives too quickly. In the minutes before sleep came for me, I had silently wished for another assignment, even if it was accompanied by terrible pain; just something to keep Rebecca with me even one day longer. But nothing came, and today is the day. We are only three hours' drive from her father's home, and today I will have to say goodbye. Words can't adequately describe how much I don't want that to happen. For a few brief seconds last night, I actually considered faking a new assignment, just to delay the inevitable, but I couldn't do that to her.

As daylight begins to fill our room, Rebecca awakens. I can tell that she is momentarily disoriented; waking up in a new place every day will do that to you. Once she remembers where she is, she looks over at me in my bed and smiles. "You stayed all night," she says.

"Where else would I go?"

"Come sit by me," she invites.

I get out of bed, still in the clothes I wore last night, and return to the chair at her bedside. "How are you feeling today?" I ask.

"I think I'm all right again. Sleep helped. And I guess whatever they're pumping into my arm did too."

"It's pudding, actually. I checked with the nurse. Intravenous pudding. Radical new treatment they're trying."

"What flavor is it? You better not say tapioca."

"No, see, they can't use tapioca, because the gooey bits clog up the tube. This is medical-grade chocolate fudge."

"No wonder I'm feeling better. That always made me feel better when I was a—" She doesn't finish the sentence. The memory has clearly stirred others, and after last night, it's not somewhere she wants to go.

"What am I going to do?" she asks.

"That's up to you. Right now, nobody in your family knows you're coming. You could go back to your father's house. Or you could go live with your mother. Or ... you could travel with me."

"I couldn't do that. I couldn't leech off of you all the time."

"You wouldn't be leeching. You'd be working with me. Everything you've done so far has helped me. And I like having you with me."

"I'm so afraid to face my father ... but I have to know. I have to know what really happened and why he made the decisions he did. He buried the truth for so long. Now I need to know why. Would you be upset with me if I asked you to take me home?"

"Of course not. It was the original plan anyway. Just as long as you're sure this is what you want to do."

"I'm as sure as I'll get," she tells me.

"Then let's get you there."

127

The hospital graciously allows us to take showers, something we haven't done in more than thirty hours, even after all the work we did. The warm water and a fresh change of clothes feel good. I keep waiting for the other shoe to drop and a new assignment to come in, but it doesn't. Maybe this recent outbreak of back-to-back assignments really is an anomaly, and I can look forward to a few days of peace at a time.

We pause long enough to have breakfast in the hospital cafeteria. Clichéd jokes about hospital food aside, it's really quite satisfying and very much needed.

"Thank you for bringing me here last night," she says.

"I was worried about you. I know enough first aid to know that you were alive and you needed someone who knew a lot more. This was the closest hospital."

"What did they say when you told them we'd been in Wyandotte?"

"Not surprisingly, they asked why. I told them we were doing a report on the town and that seemed to end that line of questioning, but it was clear from the doctor's attitude that Wyandotte still has a reputation as a health risk. Your situation just adds to that perception."

"Do you think the place will ever be inhabitable again?" she asks.

"If enough people make an effort, and there's a whole lot of money put into it, then maybe. The things that poisoned that town tend to last, but the earth is good at healing. Eighteen years is a long time."

"I remember things now—things from my childhood, from before the smog. I was very young, but I have so many positive memories. All this time, I never knew the town's name. My birth certificate says I was born in Pittsburgh."

"Well, maybe when you're a big-time lawyer, you can make Wyandotte a pet project."

"Yeah," she replies, "maybe I can."

"I hate to be indelicate at this tender moment, but after breakfast, we need to get out of this place. I didn't want to look for an insurance card last night, so I told them I'd get it from you this morning."

"Oh," she says. "Yeah. An insurance card."

"Shall I infer from your repetition of those words that you don't have an insurance card?"

"Well, they kinda don't give you one if you don't have insurance."

"Fair enough. Come on, let's head to the business office."

I pay for her treatment on my credit card. She protests but quickly realizes that without my generosity, she's somewhat stuck, so she accepts.

"I'm going to find a way to pay you back," she insists as we make our way to the hospital's parking garage.

"Consider it worker's comp. You were injured on the job."

"I was *injured*," she corrects, "by going back to my family home, someplace I had no business going."

We get into the car and exit the garage, with the top down and me behind the wheel. The conversation continues. "I would've done the same thing," I tell her. "If I knew I was that close to my childhood home, I would have wanted to see it. Even in the condition it was in."

"Once I was inside, it didn't feel like my home. And it wasn't just the destruction. I just felt like I didn't belong there."

"I'm sorry, Rebecca. I brought you there, opened up all those old wounds. I would never have asked you to come along if I knew the connection."

"Yeah," she says, "the connection. Don't you think we're seeing a lot of those?"

"Yes, I do. At first, I thought it was coincidence, but there's just too many of them. The only thing that's missing for me is an explanation. You have to leave Key West, because you're in some danger if you stay there. We end up in Marathon, in Casner's room, so it's possible that Casner was the danger, but we don't know why. Then I get the assignment to go to Atlanta to save Casner."

"But if he was the reason I was in danger," she rightly points out, "why would we go to Atlanta to save him?"

"A fair question. One of many I can't answer at this point. Then we head to Wyandotte, which just happens to be your childhood home. It seems to me that all these coincidences started when I picked you up."

"So I'm the key to all of this?"

"I don't know, but it sure feels like it. But for every connection, there's a disconnect. A piece of the puzzle that doesn't fit with the rest. Your father, for instance."

"Shit, that reminds me—I still haven't called him to tell him I'm coming home."

"Do you want me to pull over so you can have some privacy?"

"I don't need privacy, but it'll be easier with the top up. Can you pull over just long enough for me to make the call?"

I find a safe spot to pull to the side of the road and put the top up. Rebecca gets her cell phone out and stares at it for a few seconds, finding the courage to make the call.

"Not too late to change your mind," I remind her.

"Thank you," she replies. She dials the number from memory—hers, not the phone's—and waits patiently as it rings. I can see the apprehension on her face. "Hi, Daddy. It's Rebecca." I can't hear what he's saying; all I can do is gauge it based on her words and her reactions. She looks very tense. "I'm sorry I haven't talked to you in so long. I've been busy." I watch as she listens. "I've been working hard to save up some money.… I know, but it was important to me. I have something to tell you, and I'm sorry that it's kind of short notice. I've decided to go back to school." She appears to be bracing herself for his reaction. "Well, that's why I'm calling you. I'm on my way home now. I'm less than three hours away.…" Is he pleased to hear this? I can't tell by her face. I try hard not to stare, but it's almost impossible. "I'd really appreciate it if I could stay with you for a few days until I can get living arrangements settled on campus.… Thank you, Daddy. Sorry it's such short notice." She looks at me and nods; apparently, Daddy approves. "No, it's fine. I'll be arriving by car.… A friend is taking me home.… It's no one you know; it's someone I met in Florida. That's where I've been living, Florida.… Well, I should go so we can finish the drive. Thank you for letting me stay. I'll give you all the news when I get there.… See you soon. Bye."

And there it is. No sentimentality, no real emotion at all from either side. Just *see you soon.* "Are you all right?" I ask her.

"Yeah, it's fine. Put the top down again, would you? I could use the air."

She seems fine, maybe too fine. But I don't want to pry, so I lower the top and merge back onto the highway. After a minute or two of silence, she turns to me and says, "Tell me about the first time you got an assignment to help somebody."

"Well, it started with the message, like it always does. I thought it was strange, but I didn't think too much of it. But then the pain started, and it didn't go away for hours. I even went to a doctor. He asked me all kinds of questions, then did test after test, and couldn't find anything wrong with me physically. Not even a morphine shot took the pain away. I was just about ready to talk to a psychiatrist, but then I decided I would pass the message on to the person who needed to hear it, and see what happened."

"So who was this person?" she asks.

"It was a friend of mine; why?"

"I'm looking for connections. With everything that's gone on, I want to see if your first assignment has some connection to me. What's your friend's name?"

"Esteban Padgett."

"Esteban Padgett?" she repeats, her voice full of disbelief.

"Yes. Do you know him?"

"No, never heard of him, but that's a really weird name, don't you think?"

"I don't know, Persephone Traeger, you tell me."

"Touché, Tristan Shays. Now that we're all done making fun of each other's name, let's see if we can find a connection. Where was Esteban?"

"Maryland," I reply.

"Maryland," she says. "I've never been there. Oh my gosh, is that where you live?"

"Yes."

"It just occurred to me that in the past four days that we've known each other, I've never asked you where you live or really anything about yourself. So you live in Maryland. Where?"

"Ocean City."

"I love the name. It sounds like a great place."

"It is. I wish I could spend more time there than I do."

"Do you have a big house overlooking the Atlantic?"

I smile a bit at her accuracy. "Yes, I actually do."

"I'm picturing gray wooden siding and white shutters, and a long ramp that leads down to a little stretch of beach all your own," she says playfully.

"Go on," I say, now gently uneasy.

"In the living room, there's a brick fireplace with a big mantel. Across the room is a stairway leading to the second floor." By this point, she's no longer asking me, she's telling me. "Upstairs, your bedroom has french doors that lead to a wraparound balcony that circles the entire second floor. Tristan, how is this possible? How can I know this?"

"Because I'm picturing each part of the house just before you describe it."

"What?"

"Twenty questions," I say suddenly.

"What?"

"Twenty questions. Right now."

"This is no time for games."

"On the contrary, I think it's a very good time for games. You guess first. It's a person."

"This is scaring me, Tristan."

"Put the fear aside and focus. It's a person."

"Is it a man?" she asks, nowhere near in the spirit of the game.

"Yes."

"Is he over fifty?"

"Yes."

"Is it Sean Connery?"

"Yes, Rebecca, it is."

She is almost in tears, not from happiness over her easy win, but with the uncertainty of what it means.

"Keep going," I say to her. "A place this time."

"Is it a city?"

"Yes."

"Is it Rio de Janeiro?"

"Yes. I'm thinking of an ordinary playing card from a deck. What is it?"

"Ten of hearts?"

"Yes. Another one."

"Four of clubs?"

"Right again. One more."

"Ace of clubs."

I look at her with renewed wonder. "A-plus."

She doesn't share my fascination. "Why is this happening?"

"It seems, my lovely Rebecca, that you *are* with me for a reason. You have a gift as well, one that's getting stronger now."

"What if I don't want that gift?"

My wonder turns to sympathy; she is genuinely overwhelmed at this revelation, and she needs a friend right now. "I'm not sure," I answer, holding her hand in mine. "Sometimes it's something you can bury down deep in your thoughts, and sometimes it just needs to be heard. It's clear that you have a very strong connection to me, but that might not be the case with everyone. After all, you and I have gotten quite close in the past four days. What about with other people? Were you able to hear the Harbisons' thoughts, or the staff at the hospital?"

"No, I don't think I was."

"Open yourself up right now to anyone nearby. See if you can hear any of the other people around us."

She closes her eyes tightly and squints in concentration. After several seconds, she reports, "All I can hear is you, and I couldn't hear everything. It's like I could hear what you wanted me to hear."

"That's good. It means you're very focused. You won't spend your life shutting out the thoughts of others."

"Tristan, this is all so sudden …"

"Maybe it is and maybe it isn't. I think this might be something you've been able to do for years, a latent ability that got stronger the more time you spent with me. Think back to the night we met. What motivated you to ask me to drive you home?"

"Convenience, I guess."

"I was a stranger to you. Or was I? In your mind, did you see me as a threat or as something else?"

She thinks back. "You represented safety. How is it that I'm realizing this now, but I didn't at the time when I made the decision to go with you?"

"At the time, you realized it subconsciously. Now, that thought and a lot more are in your consciousness."

"So why do I have these numbers going through my head?"

"Numbers? When did this start?"

"When I woke up this morning, they were in there. Now they're starting to repeat themselves."

"What are the numbers?"

"Twenty-eight, ten, sixteen, N. Eighty-three, five, eleven, W. Hey, do you think they're lottery numbers? Do you think somebody wants me to win the lottery?"

"I'd love to say you're right, but those letters in there make me think otherwise. Do you have a pen and paper in your purse?"

"Yeah."

"Write the numbers down and read them to me again."

She gets the pen and paper and writes down what she had told me. "Twenty-eight, ten, sixteen, N. Eighty-three, five, eleven, W. What does it mean?"

"Unless this is some kind of cryptic code, N means north."

"And W means west," she deduces. "Latitude and longitude?"

"Might very well be. I don't have an atlas in the car, so I can't say where those points meet."

"Wait a second," she interrupts. "My cell phone has a GPS application on it. I can enter those coordinates and see where it takes us." She types in the numbers and we wait, all the while making our way westward into Ohio. After many seconds of waiting, she tells me, "It has an answer. It's in the Gulf of Mexico."

"*In* the gulf?"

"Yeah, that's what it says."

"Can you tell where specifically?"

"Western coast of Florida ... about ten miles off the coast of—"

"What? What is it?"

"Tarpon Springs," she says.

A prolonged moment of silence passes between us as we both try to understand the significance of what this means. Tarpon Springs, one piece that didn't fit into the puzzle before, now tries to squeeze into place. But ten miles offshore? What could be out there?

"It's important to know where these numbers are coming from," I tell her. "Does it feel like they're coming from me?"

"No. Your thoughts sound like you, like your voice. These aren't like that. It doesn't feel like I'm hearing them, like someone's speaking them or thinking them. I'm just ... *aware* of them. They're a presence, and I don't know why."

"I wonder if your father might be the key to any of this. When we get there, do you think you could try to read his thoughts?"

"I don't know. I guess I could. You think he's sending me these numbers?"

"You said it's getting stronger the closer we get to his house. That would suggest that someone in that area is sending them to you, and he's the logical candidate."

She looks very uncomfortable with that possibility, and I don't blame her. Though her relationship with her father has been strained for some time, the more she learns about him, the unhappier she becomes.

Crossing the border into Ohio, I exit the interstate and turn onto a state highway that will take us the remaining ninety miles to her father's house. Traffic is much lighter here, making it easier for us to talk and to think.

"Do you want me to drive for a while?" she asks.

"No, I'm fine. You're still recuperating. I'll take us the rest of the way."

"I feel fine, really. A hundred percent better than I did last night."

"Good. Then it's a lovely day to be a passenger. Sit back and relax. I've got this covered."

"Relax, right. Easy for you to say. I find out I'm a mind reader who's getting coordinates in my head for no apparent reason."

"Gotta keep a positive attitude. Find ways to use this to your advantage. Won't it be nice to know what your professors are thinking? Or to know if a first date has something unsavory on his mind?"

She looks at me for many seconds. "You really want me to go, don't you?"

Now it's my turn to be confused. "I thought that was the whole idea of this trip. I take you home, you go back to school. Did I miss the part where that changed?"

"I thought you would at least try to talk me out of leaving."

"Rebecca, I ..."

"Sure, the night we met, I said I wanted you to drive me there, but now ... Everything we've been through— We've made love."

"I know. I was there."

"Was it just a one-night stand? Just some conquest?"

"No, of course not. Rebecca, it was … it was beautiful, and it brought us closer in a way that nothing else could have. Right now, I'm a victim of geography. Unless you know a scenic route to your father's house through Alabama, we're going to be there in less than two hours. And I don't think your idea of romance involves a quickie in a rest area. For someone who has the ability to read my thoughts, you're certainly missing the biggest one—the one where I'd do just about anything to keep you from leaving this car and walking out of my life forever."

And there it is, out in the open. I guess I am a bit surprised seconds later when she quietly says, "I *did* know. I just needed to hear you say it."

I laugh a little to myself and shake my head. "You're impossible. You do know this, right?"

"So what are we going to do?" she asks.

"I don't know. As long as these assignments continue, I have to keep moving."

"Would you come see me in between?"

"I'd really like that. Because you mean a whole lot more to me than a one-night stand. I really think I—"

My thoughts are interrupted as I glance down the road ahead. On the side of the highway, a car is parked with its hazard lights flashing. I see a male figure standing in our lane, waving his arms for us to stop.

"Is that a cop?" Rebecca asks me.

At first I'm willing to believe it, but as we draw closer, I recognize the figure and know that this is no member of law enforcement. Rebecca recognizes him as well.

"That's impossible," I say aloud.

"What would he be doing here?" she asks.

I slow the car to a stop, and the figure approaches. With no pause for greetings or formalities, he gets right to the point. "My friends, you have to come with me," he says through his thick accent.

"Stelios, what are you doing here?" I ask him. "How did you find us?"

"There's no time. Follow me to the next town. There is a little café where we can have some privacy. I'll explain everything there. Hurry. It's not safe if we're seen talking here."

Chapter 12

Without another word of explanation, Stelios hurries back to his car, gets in, and pulls into the lane ahead of us. Rebecca and I exchange a perplexed glance, simultaneously wondering if we should actually follow him, and then decide to do so. He drives fast, and I pace him, not wanting to lose him. As promised, he gets off at the next exit and we follow, down the off-ramp, around a corner, through several intersections to a tiny café in a quiet portion of a small town whose name I didn't even catch. I park and put the top back up, then we follow him into the building.

Stelios catches a waiter's eye, and the young man waves us back to a little meeting room with three tables in it in the back of the café. We all sit down together. "Are you hungry?" Stelios asks us. "Can I get you anything?"

Rebecca shakes her head. "No," I tell him.

He turns to the waiter. "Bring us a pitcher of water and three glasses."

The server exits, leaving us alone. "How did—"

Stelios holds up one hand, motioning for me to stop. The waiter enters the room and pours three glasses of water.

"We are not to be disturbed," Stelios tells him, handing him twenty dollars.

The waiter takes the money. "Yes, sir."

"By *anyone*."

137

"Yes, sir." He exits swiftly and once again we have privacy.

"You must have many questions," Stelios says.

"That's putting it mildly," I reply. "For starters, how did you find us? Have you been following us?"

"In a manner of speaking, yes. Your thought patterns are very distinctive, Tristan. Yours as well, Persephone. After we met, I was able to track you. I could tell where you were and where you were going. Just as I know where it is you're going now. That's why I had to talk to you before you get there. So I caught a flight last night and rented a car. And here we all are, together again," he says pleasantly.

"Why us?" Rebecca asks. "Why is this happening?"

He looks squarely at her and the pleasantness leaves his voice. "How well do you know your father?" She looks away from him, forgetting how deep inside of her Stelios can see. "You've been to Wyandotte. You learned the truth about that place. About what he did there. But do you know about Consolidated Offshore?"

The name doesn't sound familiar to me, and Rebecca shows no recognition either. "No," she says. "What is it?"

"Consolidated Offshore is a group of oil speculators from all over the country. Men who have some money to invest, in the hopes of making much more. So they work with oil companies and geologists to search the coastal areas for the best places to drill. A few months ago, a small group of these investors was having no luck finding viable sites where they could drill. One of them had a side interest that he shared with the others—psychic ability. Do you know what dowsing is?"

I answer, "It's the ability to find water underground with the use of divining rods."

"Not just water, Tristan. Gems, minerals, anything hidden within the earth. Scientists try to say that dowsing is a fraud, that it doesn't work. That's because in order to make it work, the dowsers need to have some psychic ability, and this flies in the face of science. This group turned to dowsers to try to find the oil, and in the past month, they believe they've found a significant source of it."

"But that's good news ... isn't it?" Rebecca asks.

"Good news for them, certainly. If they strike oil there, it will be a windfall. But every discovery comes at a price. The area where they are planning to drill is in the Gulf of Mexico, just ten miles—"

"Off the coast of Tarpon Springs," Rebecca says, finishing his sentence.

"Very good, Persephone."

She gets a far-off look. "Twenty-eight degrees, ten minutes, sixteen seconds north; eighty-three degrees, five minutes, eleven seconds west."

"Thank you for those coordinates," he says, quickly writing them down. "I didn't have an exact location until now. Do you know what is at twenty-eight degrees, ten minutes, sixteen seconds north; eighty-three degrees, five minutes, eleven seconds west?"

"No."

"My fishing grounds, dear Persephone. Mine and my friends'. Hundreds of fishermen, looking for fish, shellfish, sponges—all creatures that will be wiped out if Consolidated Offshore begins drilling operations there as planned."

"What does this have to do with my father?"

"Calvin Traeger is one of the investors using dowsers to find sites. He's one of the backers for the Tarpon Springs drill site."

She rests her head in her hands in disbelief.

Stelios continues, "He must have had one of his people send you those coordinates to keep them safe, in case something happened to him."

"It makes sense now," I tell him. "You knew we were going to see him, and you want us to ask him not to drill there, because of your fishing grounds."

"I wish it were that simple, Tristan. This has gone far beyond polite conversation and personal appeals. There is a war going on, and the two of you are caught in the middle of it. I came here today to stop you from going there at all. You'll be safest if you're nowhere near Calvin Traeger or anything he touches."

"No ..." Rebecca says. I reach out a hand to calm her.

"Stelios, you don't understand," I say. "I was sent to get her, to take her home, because she was in danger if she stayed in Florida."

"And where did you get that message?" he asks calmly.

"The same place I've been getting them for the past two years."

"And where is that? From heaven? From God? Would you know a true message from a false one, Tristan?"

"A false one? I don't understand."

"You are a messenger. You and a handful of others like you go about helping others, just as you did with me. And for this, I thank you. But this gift of yours … it marks you. There are others out there who know you have this ability, and they can manipulate you, make you do their will by making you believe that the assignment comes from above. This is why you were sent to get Persephone. Her father needs her home again. So he instructed one of his team members to reach out and project an assignment to a vulnerable messenger. And you received that message, thinking it was real."

"Are you saying I was used?"

"Yes, you were. Persephone here is very valuable to her father's work. You're discovering that Tristan isn't the only one with gifts, aren't you, my lovely little friend?"

"Yes," she answers quietly.

"These gifts of yours will help your father. He doesn't have them himself, but the same associate who saw Tristan's abilities must have been able to see yours as well. And now he wants you to help him find the oil. This is why you were summoned home. You weren't in danger before, but if you join with him, you will be. There are those who will go to great lengths to protect their livelihood."

"Stop it," I say sternly. "You're scaring her."

"She needs to be scared. I can't guarantee the safety of her father or anyone in his investment group. If you doubt me, ask Jeffrey Casner."

The name sends a shiver up my spine. "Casner … He was one of them?"

Stelios nods. "A major investor in the group, with ties to organized crime."

"But I don't understand. I was sent to warn him about the car bomb."

He sighs deeply. "I owe you an apology, my friend. The one who sent you to Atlanta to talk to Casner was me."

"You? But …"

"I sent you there because I needed someone to take the blame. When I met you and Persephone, I was able to see who she was. I saw the connection to Calvin Traeger, and I couldn't take a chance. I sent you there in enough time to talk to Casner, but I knew you wouldn't convince him."

"How could you possibly know that?"

"Because I called him ahead of time and bullied him. Told him he was a coward and he would back down from any threats. I also kept him from completing his vacation plans that day."

At last I reach my breaking point. I spring from my seat and grab Stelios by the lapels—the second time, I realize, I have done this to someone in the past three days, and probably the second time in my life. "You son of a bitch! They arrested me for murder! They thought I killed Casner."

"I know," he says calmly, and once again I am dismayed at how calm people are when I grab them by the lapels. I really need to work on my fierceness. "They thought exactly what I wanted them to think. I am sorry."

"You're sorry? Oh, well, that makes it all better then, doesn't it?"

"You can hit me if it will make you feel better," he says, still calm. "But please try to see it from my point of view. You arrive on my boat with my enemy's daughter, and I can sense that she is a psychic. You tell me that my boat is going to sink. How could I see you as anything other than a threat?"

"We came to warn you," I remind him. "We came to save you from having that very thing happen to you, and this is how you repaid us?"

"After Atlanta, I realized that I had misjudged you. Believe me, I was quite relieved to see that you had been released from custody. Tristan, I really regret putting you in that situation. That is why I came here now, to warn you not to finish your journey."

I release him and pace around the table a bit. "So you killed Casner?" I ask.

"No. The people who did that are far away from here, and they mean you no harm. Casner's death was a warning to other members of the cartel."

"Like my father?" Rebecca chimes in, quite agitated.

"Yes."

"So they're going to kill him next?" she asks.

"I honestly don't know. I wasn't exaggerating when I told you this

141

is a war. There are those on both sides who will do whatever it takes to prevail."

"Now that I know this, what's to stop me from going to the Atlanta Police and telling them about your part in Casner's murder?" I ask.

"Because I think you will look deep inside yourself and realize that I truly am on your side in all of this. And … although I would hate to do so, I have gathered pieces of evidence which, if given to the police, would very convincingly implicate young Persephone here in the murder. You have an alibi; she does not."

Rebecca and I share a glance that says we both believe he means it.

"As I said, I don't want to do that. All you have to do is go your way and let me go mine. The world will not miss Jeffrey Casner …"

"No, but I suspect his wife will," I interrupt.

"Less than you might think," he says. "He has inflicted hurt upon her, both physical and emotional. There are some men in the world for whom no one will grieve."

At last, after all the questions I've had these past four days, the answer is standing before me, telling me everything I need to know, and I am completely unprepared to accept what he is saying. It's too much; it's just too much to take. The knowledge that other people can send me on their own little assignments sickens me; how many times have I fallen for it, thinking that I was serving a higher authority? All along, I've been feeling enormously guilty, believing I'd dragged Rebecca into this whole thing. Now I realize that, in fact, she dragged *me* into this whole thing, however unwittingly, and I don't know how to feel about that. I can't blame her and I can't abandon her now, so close to the end. But Stelios keeps using the word *war,* and it feels ominously like a major battleground awaits us on Calvin Traeger's doorstep.

"I'm not your enemy," Rebecca tells Stelios, in response to his earlier threat.

"I know that now. You didn't choose your family; and you were wise to get as far away from them as possible. The best thing you can do now is to do just that. Go back to Key West if you'd like. Or California, or Europe. But don't tell them where you are going or why. You can bet that if I know of your gifts, others know of them too—others who would consider you their enemy. Or at least a weapon against their enemy."

She shoots him an icy glare. "I want to hate you for this."

"I will understand if you do."

The tension is building between them, and I have to I interrupt it. "How widespread is it? This psychic phenomena ... I mean, three of us in this room. How far does it go?"

Stelios looks surprised at the question. "It's everywhere. Every person alive has the potential to do what we do. Most of them don't know it, and enough of them actively disbelieve it, so for the most part, it lies dormant. The devoutly religious are skeptical of such things, so they attribute their gifts to divine inspiration, and that makes them happy. Others call it coincidence and don't pursue it any further. But there are still plenty who do use it."

"But if it's out there, why isn't the media all over this? This would be huge news."

"Every now and then, the press gets wind of it, but it gets written off as a human interest story. Everyone says *isn't that nice,* and they go about their business."

"There's a man who'll pay a million dollars to anyone who can demonstrate verifiable paranormal activity ..."

Stelios laughs. "Oh yes, big man. You should see the conditions he sets forth in order to claim the prize. It's like putting someone on a toilet standing on their head, with their fingers in their ears and raccoons balanced on their feet, and telling them they'll get a million dollars if they can take a shit that comes out purple and looks like Abraham Lincoln."

Rebecca laughs at the mental image. "Pardon my language," Stelios says to her. *Ever the gentleman.*

"Psychic ability is out there, Tristan, and people are using it."

"So why aren't all these psychics winning the lottery with their abilities?" I ask him.

"Who the hell do you think *is* winning the lottery? Do you know what the odds are of picking those numbers by chance, without cheating? You show me a lottery winner, and I'll show you a psychic. But there aren't many who can do it ... because most of us don't have control over our gifts. We fuss and we fumble and we try to make sense of it when we get glimpses of the future or we know what someone else is thinking. The strongest of us have control. The rest do what we can."

"So how do I know if the assignments I get are real or if someone is using me, manipulating me for their own purposes?"

His answer is brief and direct: "You don't."

"How do I know you're telling the truth now," I ask him, "about any of this?"

"Ask Persephone. She's been reading my thoughts since we entered this room. Words can lie, but thoughts will always tell the truth."

I turn to Rebecca and she nods. "It's true."

"So I'm at their mercy, whoever they are."

"Yes," he says.

"And her? What happens to her now?"

Before he can reply, Rebecca interrupts. "Tristan, it's fine. My eyes are open now, about a lot of things. I understand that meeting you was important. Maybe this all happened for a reason, maybe it didn't. But it happened, and we have to live with it." She walks over to Stelios, standing right in front of him, and says to his face, "Blaming Stelios won't help anything."

I watch as she stares directly into his eyes for five seconds, then ten, then fifteen. He stares back at her and then he nods at her—discreetly, but it is enough that I can see it. After that, she steps away from him; I can only wonder what silent communication they have shared.

She turns to me. "We have to go."

"My friends," Stelios says, "I truly am sorry for any harm I have caused you. I hope you stay safe and well, and I hope you make the right decision. You won't see me or hear from me again, unless you seek me out."

I can't bring myself to say goodbye to him. Despite all his apologies and all his contrition, I can't forgive him for what he did to me in Atlanta. I leave that little room, with Rebecca following close behind, neither of us giving a backward glance.

We return to the Sebring and both of us move toward the driver's door. "Give me the keys, please," she says.

"Why?"

"I need to drive us. I need to focus on something to get past everything that's in my head right now."

I hand her the keys and make my way to the passenger's side, climbing into the seat. She opens the driver's side, starts the engine, and lowers the top. Without signaling, she makes a U-turn and heads quickly back through town, back to the highway. Her face holds an inscrutable concentration and intensity, and without her gift, I don't know her thoughts or her plans. After two minutes of silence, I have to ask her, "Where are we going?"

"Where are we going?" she repeats, sounding annoyed at the question. "We're going to my father's house. Where else would we be going?"

"But you heard what Stelios said ... "

"I heard *exactly* what he said. He said there are people out there who want to kill my father, and he might not even know it. I have to warn him that he's in danger."

"Then call him and tell him! Rebecca, if you go there, you'll be in danger too. You have a phone, you have his number. Call him."

To my great surprise, she turns on me, shouting at me with an anger I've never seen in her. "How fucking dare you tell me to call him! You of all people? This is what you do, Tristan. You put your own safety aside and travel all over the country to warn people you've never even met that they're in danger. This is my father! I have to look him in the eye and tell him what could happen. And right now, I don't care what he's done or what he's planning to do. They don't get to kill him for it. Not for oil or zinc or ... or a bunch of God damn fish!"

Her words are carried off by the wind, and I see such pain in her eyes as she struggles not to dissolve into tears. In the aftermath of her fury, my argument seems weak, completely without merit. We *are* on an assignment, only this time, she is the messenger, and I am along for the ride.

"I'm sorry," I say quietly. "You're absolutely right, and I have no business questioning your judgment. I let my own fear for your safety cloud my thinking. You need to go there and face him and tell him what you know. And if I can help, I will. And if I can't help, I'll stand back and let you do what you have to do."

To my surprise, she slows the car and pulls over onto the shoulder, putting it in park. With a flood of exhaustion-induced tears, she leans over and throws her arms around me, sobbing out her words. "I'm sorry I yelled. I'm sorry for all of it. I'm just so scared, and I don't know what to do. I don't know if this is the right thing to do."

"It's the right thing," I answer. "If it's what your heart needs, then it's the right thing."

"These last four days have ripped away everything I considered normal in my life. I miss my friends, and I miss my classes, and I even miss my father."

"Then take us to him, Rebecca. We're almost there. This assignment is yours to complete."

She composes herself and puts us back on the road, on the final leg of our journey. "Tristan, I'm so sorry that they tricked you into coming all that way to get me."

"I'm not. Don't you know that meeting you was the best thing that's happened to me since this whole thing started two years ago?"

"No ... I didn't know."

I laugh, feeling a bit choked up. "And you call yourself a mind reader," I tease.

She laughs too and slaps my arm. "Shut up. I'm new at this."

The miles pass quickly as the two of us regain our inner peace and try to focus on the task ahead. She takes us down familiar roads as we enter the metropolitan area of Dayton, Ohio. We drive through suburb after suburb, each getting a bit fancier than the last. Rebecca signals a turn onto a road leading into the village of Palisade Heights. "This is it, isn't it?" I ask.

She nods. "Less than two miles now."

"Are you all right?"

"No," she says, "but I'm here. And I have to do this."

"Solidarity," I reply, taking her hand in mine. "I'm here for you."

She drives on, and in three minutes, we are turning onto Leighton Terrace, a street lined with expensive homes. In the distance, on the right, I see three police cars parked in front of a house, with six officers out of their cars, seemingly standing guard with the homeowner. "Is that your father's house?" I ask.

"Yes," she says. "I wonder why all the police are there."

"Maybe he learned about the threat and they're keeping him safe. Go ahead and pull up and we'll ask him."

She parks at the curb, as close to the house as she can get, and we both get out of the car. Rebecca hurries past the police perimeter undisturbed and goes right to her father. He's a good-looking, well-dressed man in his late forties, with an air of self-assurance that hangs about him like overpriced cologne. He looks like trouble, plain and simple. It doesn't take me long to realize how right I am. I lag behind a bit, but when I reach the officers furthest down the driveway, two of them each put a hand on my shoulders. Before I can even ask what's going on, they bring me over to one of their cars and search me for weapons, finding none.

"He's secure," one of them tells Rebecca's father.

"Keep him there," Calvin Traeger replies.

Rebecca hugs her father briefly, and then asks him, "Daddy, what's going on? Why are these men here?"

"I had to make sure you were safe, honey. These men are here to help us." He is right on the verge of earning my respect for saying that, but then he turns to the cop who's got me and says, "All right, you can take him away."

"Take who away?" I answer. "Take *me* away?"

Rebecca protests. "No, Daddy—why?"

"Kidnapping," he says, and the word clearly sounds as absurd to Rebecca as it does to me.

"You can't be serious!" I say to him.

"You took my daughter from her workplace and drove her across the country. I'm prepared to press charges."

"I brought her home to you. That's why we're here. I know you had one of your people send me to tell her to come back home." Two cops hold me back and keep me from presenting my argument directly to Traeger. So I tell the officers, "There's no kidnapping here. She asked me to drive her here and I did. For God's sake, look who was driving the car when we pulled up! Kidnappers typically don't take shifts with their victims."

They look to Traeger, who maintains a stony silence, so they don't release me. Rebecca takes up the charge. "Please let him go. He didn't kidnap me or hurt me or anything like that. This man is my friend. I asked him to drive me here and he did."

To our mutual amazement, nothing happens. In any normal situation, a statement like that from the supposed victim would at least give the arresting officers reason to ease up on the suspect, and yet these men don't. The realization dawns on Rebecca. "Since these officers aren't moving after hearing that, I guess there's no point in talking to them, is there? I guess I need to talk to the person who's paying them." She turns back to her father. "Is this the way you want things? You make me come back here, then show me that I can't trust you. How will that help anything?"

"You'll trust me because I'm your father, and I'm looking out for your best interests."

"I don't believe you. You've never looked out for anyone's best interests but your own. Why do you think I was so eager to leave home in the first place? I've been to Wyandotte this week. I talked to people who lived through the smog. I know what you did there ..."

"Rebecca, Wyandotte was an unfortunate natural disaster caused by the weather. The plant wasn't producing anything it hadn't produced every day of every year of its existence. Did your new friends tell you what the plant was helping to manufacture? Protective gear for the United States military. How many lives would have been lost if we had shut down that plant at the first sign of bad weather?"

"I know about Consolidated Offshore too, Dad," she adds, trying to stay strong.

He maintains a look of composure, but he is clearly surprised by this. He tells her, "Consolidated is our chance to start a new life ... with your help."

"*My* help?"

"You have skills I need to be successful, Rebecca. You'll live at home with me, help me run the company by day, and take business classes at the college at night."

"That's not why I'm here," she says. "I came home to go back to school full time during the day and take law classes."

"It's not up to you," he says calmly. "You know how we operate: my house, my rules."

"Well, it doesn't have to be your house, your rules," she says defiantly. "I'm not a child anymore. I can live on campus; I can pay my own tuition if I have to."

"Yes, that's true. And I can call the dean's office and tell them where you got that tuition money. How do you think that would sit with them? With a board of directors that's made up mostly of church elders? Do you think they'd welcome you back and accept money you've made by parading your naked body in front of deviants and lowlifes? Don't look so surprised, Rebecca. You're not the only one who knows things. In order to find you and bring you here, I had to learn where you were and what you were doing. And you can bet we're going to have a very long talk about it."

"Daddy, this is crazy. Listen to yourself talk. You have to stop what you're doing with Consolidated. You're in danger if you don't. There are people who will protect their interests any way they can. They killed Jeffrey Casner in Atlanta."

"I know that. I also know Casner was careless and overconfident. That's how they were able to get to him. But look around you. Six off-duty Palisade Heights police officers, working as my personal security force. They'll protect me and they'll protect you. Now that you're home again, I won't let anything happen to you."

"What about Tristan?" she asks.

"Who?"

I wave. "Hello."

"Ah, yes, the kidnapper," he says dismissively. *I wish he'd stop calling me that.*

"Daddy, stop it. You know it's not true."

"Mr. Traeger, please," I say to him, "this isn't what it seems. I want to clear up this misunderstanding. I swear to you, I never meant Rebecca any harm. The fact of the matter is … I love her."

Words are funny things. Sometimes they have a will of their own, and despite everything reasonable and sensible in you that knows not to say them, you open your mouth, and damned if they don't just tumble out. *I love her.* Such little words, so seemingly harmless. I look around after those words tumble. Two of the cops look as if they find it terribly sweet. Rebecca wears a look of astonishment. And Calvin Traeger sustains the same impenetrable calm he's held since the moment we arrived.

"You love her," he says, taking a step or two toward me, "is that what you said? You're telling me that you love my twenty-one-year-old daughter who you met four days ago."

And in an instant, calm turns to rage. Without a hint of warning, Calvin Traeger breaks into a run, with fires of hatred burning in his eyes. I watch in amazement as he grabs a gun from one of the officers and stops inches in front of me, the gun primed and pointed right at my face.

Trying to maintain bladder control, I wait for the expected words from any of the assembled law enforcement officers—*Put the gun down* or *Don't do it, Mr. Traeger* or even *Let's be reasonable about this.* But they are clearly paid quite well, and not one of them makes a sound or a move in my defense.

Rebecca alone sounds the alarm. "Daddy, no!"

"Well, you listen to me," he growls at me through clenched teeth. "You don't love my daughter. I do."

"Love is a strong word," I say, trying to back-pedal. "I mean it in the sense of ... of ... respect and admiration. In a brotherly way, you might say. Certainly not in a way that ... that ... suggests anything inappropriate."

"I'd better not find out that there was anything inappropriate, because if there was, you know where the first shot will go."

To my astonishment, Rebecca dashes over and stands between her father and me. She grabs the hand that holds the pistol and places the gun to her own head. "There," she says, "you want to play with guns? You want to shoot someone today? Go for it, Daddy. Shoot your little whore of a daughter."

"What are you doing?" I whisper to her.

"Saving your life," she whispers back. "What were *you* doing?"

"Disregarding what turned out to be a very wise deer."

"What?"

"I'll tell you later. For now, get yourself out of here. I'm not worth risking your life over."

"Listen to him, Rebecca," Traeger says, making me wonder why we were whispering in the first place, with him only inches away.

"No, Daddy, you listen to me. This has gone far enough. I asked Tristan to drive me here because I thought I needed to go back to college. Then I found out that you were just using him to trick me into coming here to help you. I could've turned around right then and there, never even showed up here. But when I learned that people out there might be trying to find you and hurt you, I came here to warn you. Because no matter what's happened between us in the past, you're my father and I love you. And yet, here we are, and the fact that you still haven't put that gun down, even with me at the end of it, scares the hell out of me. Is this what you've become since I've been away? Someone so desperate for money that human life—the life of your own daughter—doesn't matter to you anymore?"

He doesn't answer, so she raises her voice to address the off-duty cops assembled here. "And you ... his so-called security force. In case you haven't noticed, this man is holding a gun on two unarmed, innocent people just because one of them said he loves the other. If it's not too much trouble, I'd appreciate it if one of you could do something about that."

The officer whose gun was taken steps calmly over to Calvin Traeger and retrieves his firearm without a word. Relieved to be out of that moment, I take two steps back, inviting Rebecca with me through a gentle touch on her arm. She steps back as well, and we look at her father.

"I'm leaving, Dad, and I'm not coming back. You could have done this right. You could have let me go back to school on my terms and then asked me to help you with your business in my spare time. But instead you went for trickery and coercion and guns, and because of that, you get nothing."

I'm proud of her determination as she turns away from him. An awkward silence hangs over everyone, so I decide to fill it with awkward words instead. "So, yeah. I would say 'nice to meet you,' but given the circumstances, I'll just leave it at 'we'll be on our way now.'"

Before Traeger can answer, Rebecca says to me, "No, we won't."

"What?"

"I asked you to drive me to Ohio so I could go back to school, and you did. Now that I'm here, I realize that this is what I need to do. I don't need my father's support or the approval of some board of directors. I've got the grades to get back in and the tuition money to pay for it, no matter where that money came from. Being with you this week showed me that I'm ready for this, and for that I'll always be grateful to you, Tristan." She puts her arms around me; what she's just said is so surprising, I almost forget to return the embrace.

"You're welcome," I reply, trying desperately to find any words to change her mind.

"Would you mind taking me to a friend's house not far from here? I need a place to stay for a while until I can get settled on campus."

"Umm … sure. Let's go."

As I walk with her down the driveway, back to the convertible, I feel almost dazed. I knew that I could lose her to her father today, but the possibility that she would reject him and then reject me as well never occurred to me, and it's making my head throb with pain, a pain that travels down my neck and into my shoulders, and then into—

Oh God, no … not this, not now—

But it's too late to stop it. The pain intensifies, like lightning traveling all through my body. And with it comes information, an assignment. I drop to my knees, crying out in pain, and then end up on my back, with my hands clutching my head. The urgency of this is overwhelming, like nothing I've ever felt before.

Through cloudy eyes, I see confusion all around me. The cops have backed off, probably wondering what's happening. I see Rebecca turn back to me, hear her call out my name, and then see her run to me. As she kneels down to hold on to me, I hear her father asking, "What the hell's wrong with him?"

"It's an assignment," she tells him, still holding me. "A mission. This is what happens to him when the information comes in."

I'm sure I am quite a spectacle to the seven men in that driveway, but I can't care. I'm focused on the details I'm receiving, and the feeling of Rebecca resting my head in her lap as she holds my hands and tries to keep me calm.

As more and more of the facts come in, I realize that I am starting to cry and words are coming out of my mouth. "No … no, I can't … not like this. It's too much. It's too much."

Through my tears, I look up at Rebecca, whose expression shows concern and uncertainty. The worst of the pain leaves me, and now I have the knowledge of what I have to do.

"Tristan," she says quietly, "what is it? What did it say?"

As I relate it to her, I can scarcely believe the magnitude of it myself. My throat is constricted, making my words come out barely loud enough for Rebecca to hear. "Cedarsburg, Kansas. There's 11,000 people who live there. In two days, a tornado will go through the center of town, tearing up everything it touches."

"Who's your contact?" she asks me. "Who do you have to save?"

There is sheer terror all over my face as I give her my one-word answer: "Everybody."

"Oh my God," she says, obviously understanding the enormity of this mission as well as I. Then, to my surprise, she helps me to a seated position and kneels next to me, saying, "Okay, we'll have to use the airlines to get there; driving's too risky, especially if there are tornadoes in the area. And some advance phone calls to the local police and fire departments will aid them in notifying residents. I don't know if we can convince them to do a full evacuation, but at least they'll be forewarned."

I look at her in amazement as she presents this plan. "What are you saying?"

"I'm saying the clock is ticking, mister, and 11,000 people are counting on you. Now, I actually have a friend who's a storm chaser at the University of Kansas. I can give him a call; he'll be a big help ..."

Now I'm truly confused. "But ... college?"

"One more assignment. This is a huge job, and you can't do it alone. College will still be there when we get done."

She rises and helps me to my feet.

"Where do you think you're going?" Traeger asks her. "I forbid you to go with him."

"Oh, we're *way* past forbidding, Dad. This man needs me, and I want to be with him."

"If you walk out of here now, don't plan on coming back."

"Can't think of a reason why I'd want to."

"Make no mistake, Rebecca: if I need your help in the future, I will find you."

"Thanks for the heads-up. Have fun finding your oil, and watch your back while you're at it. You've pissed off some really determined fishermen." She takes me by the hand. "Are you okay to walk?"

"I think so," I reply, still confused. "What just happened here?"

"I've essentially just told my father to go fuck himself, and he hasn't killed either one of us, so I'm calling that a success. Now we're going back to the car before he changes his mind, and we're going to go someplace and strategize about how to save those 11,000 people."

"Are you sure you want to do this?"

"What," Rebecca says, "you think I'm going to let you have all the fun?"

Printed in the United States
by Baker & Taylor Publisher Services